The
CANARY'S
SONG

NATALIE BANKS

CHAMPION BOOKS PUBLISHING COMPANY

Copyright 2018 by Natalie Banks

Champion Books Publishing Company

NATALIEBANKS.net

Printed in the United States of America

The Library of Congress has catalogued this edition as follows:
The Canary's Song/Natalie Banks

ISBN-13: 978-0-692-14888-4 paperback / 978-0-692-14889-1 Ebook

BOOKS BY
NATALIE BANKS

The Water is Wide
The Dark Room
The Canary's Song

New novel Coming Fall 2018

FOLLOW HER ON
FACEBOOK: Natalie Banks
INSTAGRAM: OfficialNatalieBanks
TWITTER: Natalie_Banks_

Go to
NATALIEBANKS.NET
to sign up for her newsletter and be
the first to hear about her new releases.

ACKNOWLEDGEMENTS

A S ALWAYS, I MUST thank my loving family who wait patiently for me when I am in a writing frenzy. Without their love and support, this novel would not be possible.

Thank you Joe, Caroline, Ethan, Elisabeth, Jesseca, and Jake, you guys are my world.

I have to thank my amazing editing team, Michelle Reber (I'd be lost without you!), Sue Soeres with SJS Editing Services, and last but not least, my amazing father, Jim Banks.

I also want to thank Colleen Sheehan with Ampersand Book Interiors for her pristine work on the interior formatting of my books.

Thanks also has to go to my beta reading team. These girls keep me on my toes and always make sure my novels are the best they can be. Thank you Bettina Atell, Nancy Phillips, Amy Hinshaw (my go to girl!), Rose Hevrin, Mercedes Sandford, Tricia Jones, Cynthia Banks, Michelle Young, and Kassandra Boerrigter. You guys are wonderful!

I also have to say a big thank you to Lori Beth DeHertogh, Phd. Her insight and knowledge helped this novel to be even better.

The most important thank you of all, goes to you, my readers. You all inspire me every day with your support and words of encouragement. I am thankful for each and every one of you.

Please be sure to leave me a review on Amazon and Goodreads! Your kind words are priceless to me!

The
CANARY'S
SONG

The best way out, is through.

Robert Frost

Linville Gorge Wilderness

Fish Camp

Meadow

Cabin

Mountain Vista Cabins

Country Store

CHAPTER 1

LYING IN THE DARKNESS, neither of us could speak. The knowledge of the truth laid heavily over us. I wondered if Liam felt the weight of the fear I felt? If he did, could he utter the words? I couldn't. Saying them out loud, letting them echo in the night, would only cause the scream I was holding back, to release, and I didn't know if I could ever stop.

Three weeks had passed since I had this amazing idea. To get away, just Liam and I, to a remote cabin on the edge of Linville Gorge Wilderness in the mountains of North Carolina. The promise of rekindling a relationship that had long since grown cold. No cell service, no tv, no electricity. Primitive living at its finest. It was extreme, but extreme was what we needed. The distance between us was so large, a freight train could have driven through it. I was losing him, if he wasn't gone already. Our daughter Janie was safe at my mom's house and it was only supposed to be three days.

Three days.

Three days … …

Now, I didn't know if we would be alive in 3 days, much less, ever see our daughter again.

It was the tenth of October and it was our wedding anniversary. I gave Liam a gift, a book set called Surviving in the Wilderness. It was a book filled with tips on how to survive in the wilderness. It came with a few emergency supplies, like waterproof matches, a compass, and an emergency survival blanket. I was trying to appeal to his caveman side. To lure him in, without revealing my heart's intent. I knew coming out with the truth of what I really wanted, would have just run him off. He wouldn't have given my proposal a second thought. This way, I had his attention.

With the book, I placed the reservations I had made for an amazing primitive getaway in the mountains. A place for those who wanted to get in touch with nature and solitude.

"Solitude"? he asked, as he held the reservation in his hand.

"Well, I just thought … " I couldn't finish my sentence.

We stared at each other for a long moment in silence.

"Have you already paid for this?" he almost hissed.

Trying to sound confident, I said, "Well yes, it was such a good deal because it's the off season now ... and well ... I just thought you'd really enjoy it".

He glared at me, "What about Janie?"

I took a deep breath, knowing this was a defining moment.

"My mom has offered to take her ... and it's only three days."

Once again, we just stared at each other for a moment. Then, without another word, he got up and walked out of the room.

He took the book with him, so I was cautiously hopeful.

The next morning, I was quiet.

Sulking, to be exact.

He hadn't mentioned the trip at all and I was too terrified to bring it up.

I had no idea if he was willing to go ... or if he was even considering it at all.

It was our last hope and I knew it.

Instantly, I felt a punch of bitterness in my gut.

We wouldn't be in this place, if he could have just waited a little longer for me. Why didn't he wait?

I swallowed back the tears that threatened to come. I couldn't let him see me crying.

He came into the kitchen and silently poured his morning coffee into his usual travel mug.

"I'll ask Roger to cover for me at the office." he stated emotionlessly, with his back still to me.

Relief flooded though me and I nearly jumped for joy, but instead I chose to sit motionless in the chair. I didn't want to chance even a blink of my eyes. I watched him pick up his mug and walk out the door, without a look back or even a goodbye.

Usually, I would be upset that he didn't say goodbye, but I wasn't hurt, not this time.

He said yes!

Hope swelled up in my heart and I sat quietly, letting it all soak in.

Breaking me from my euphoric trance was the sound of thundering from two little feet coming down the stairs.

"Mommmmmy!" I opened my arms and Janie ran straight into them. I hugged her and stroked the soft brown curls that fell around her face.

She looked at me with her father's green eyes, "Mommy, I want a kitty cat!" She said as she bounced up and down.

She had been asking for a cat for months. I had been in no place to answer her.

The accident.

Oh, the accident. My head spun at the thought of it.

It had been nineteen months since Jacko died and I still couldn't allow myself to think about that horrible day.

Jacko was Janie's fraternal twin brother. Babies born eight weeks early. They were fighters. The doctors weren't sure they would make it. At only three pounds each, their chances were not the best.

I remember looking at them with all those tubes and wires connected to their tiny bodies and feeling such a terror inside of me at the thought of losing either one of them. As the days passed and I watched them get stronger, that fear began to wane. I saw the strength that they both had and I knew in my heart that they would make it. I never really worried about them again. I knew they were natural born survivors.

The day they came home from the hospital was the happiest day of my life. Followed by sleepless nights, midnight feedings, loads and loads of laundry, and the most all-encompassing feeling of love that I had ever known.

Now, all that was left behind, was a huge gulley of emptiness caused by Jacko's absence. It had all but consumed us. Without him, our family wasn't the same.

I settled Janie down in front of the television with some colorful wooden building blocks and *Sesame Street*. At almost four years old, she was pretty much past the need of constant interaction.

She was always an independent child, anyway. Of the two babies, she was much less demanding. Jacko had cried more and wanted to be held incessantly.

Even at two years old and thirty pounds, he still begged to be held. I never really minded it though. It was nice to be needed.

A shudder went through my body. What I wouldn't give to hold him once more …

I walked back into the kitchen to do the morning dishes. I found myself handwashing them these days, rather than just loading the dishwasher. I found it soothing to wash the dishes by hand … warm water, bubbles, and rhythmic scrubbing, somehow took me away from the harshness of reality.

I stared out the window, as I slowly washed away oatmeal from a tiny bowl and spoon.

I was lost in memories.

It seemed so long ago that we bought this house on Sycamore Street in downtown Apex. Yet, it had only been three years. We moved in just before the babies turned one.

They had their very first birthday party in the backyard, by the pool.

The house was a green 1920's craftsman with hardwood floors and ornate mouldings. All original.

I swooned, from the moment I laid eyes on it. We had visited several homes for sale that day but the search was over the moment we turned down Sycamore Street. I knew it was "the one" immediately.

It had a red brick chimney and a lovely front porch, where we hung a white wooden swing and placed two planters with large, green ferns.

I thought about all the people who must've come in and out of this home over the years. The lives that had gone on here, long before I was even born.

I was completely enamored with the house. I fell in love with its charm and the history. I adored the wooden built-ins in the dining room and the hand carved railing that took you up the stairs to the attic room. The attic had been converted to a small bedroom, years before we had purchased the house.

One of my favorite features of the attic bedroom, was the large stained-glass window in the gable. It had an art deco design with geometric elements in green, yellow, and clear glass.

Along with the exposed rafters, it was a lovely space and we had decided right away to make that the nursery room for the babies.

Natural light poured into the whole house through the original windows. The large windows throughout the house, had four panes in the upper sash, divided by narrow vertical grids and a single-light lower pane. They gave the house a bright and happy feel even on dreary rainy days.

The people we purchased it from had completely renovated the house but thankfully had kept many of its original features. It had the best of old and new.

The house looked to me as if it had been plucked out of a magazine and placed right where it sat.

It was literally picture perfect.

It had a delightful front yard, with a lush, green carpet of grass and a mature red maple tree with vibrant leaves.

There was an inviting walkway that led from the sidewalk to the front porch. It was lined with liriope plants and lighted by a vintage lamp post.

Right after we moved in, I busied myself making it my own. I planted several azalea bushes around the front of the house, which bloomed with white flowers in the Springtime. I also placed a garden flag with a pineapple and the word WELCOME on it, next to the walkway.

The backyard was just as charming as the front. It was somewhat larger than the front yard and surrounded by a tall white picket fence. Large hydrangea bushes with giant purple blooms, grew alongside of it. There were beautiful evergreen bushes and perennial flowers planted everywhere. The previous owner spent her days in the garden and it showed.

The best feature was the oval salt water pool, in the center of the yard. A feature that Liam wasn't too thrilled about, but I loved the idea of spending the summer by the water.

On the back side of the house, a screened porch overlooked the pool. I decorated it right away, with a small wicker sofa with bright yellow cushions, a large papasan chair, and a multicolored knotted rope rug that I picked up at a flea market. I filled the rest of the space with potted plants. Beautiful lilacs, calatheas, huge white lilies, lavender, and more ferns. I hung a wind chime in the corner that would lightly ding when the wind blew in through the screens. The babies and I would sit out there for hours in nice weather. I would read while they played with their toys on the rug.

The neighborhood we lived in was filled with many other historic homes, some even older than ours. A sidewalk ran through the main part of the neighborhood, under large draping oak trees, that led you straight into the heart of downtown.

The neighborhood was picturesque with friendly neighbors and the sound of song birds.

I had walked the sidewalk many times with the babies in their dual stroller to the library for story time and to play at the park. Green Street Park was just a few blocks away from the library. We spent many lazy afternoons there. It was a lovely twelve-acre park with shade trees, a playground, soccer field, and a walking track.

Liam would join us on the weekends for these outings. We would take a picnic lunch and sit on a blanket on the grass lawn. The babies would toddle around and Liam would chase them back and forth, while they squealed with delight.

He was such a great father. I had never seen a man who loved his kids more than Liam did.

Despite his upbringing, this life suited him.

So many happy memories. We were such a perfect family.

'Were' being the key word. We *were* a perfect family.

When Jacko died, it was the beginning of the end.

The accident had rendered me nearly lifeless. Losing Jacko was beyond any pain I could ever have imagined. I withdrew from everything and everyone, including Liam and Janie. I didn't want to live, breathe or exist in a world where my baby wasn't.

At first, Liam had tried so hard to comfort me.

I would lash out and send him away. I would yell at him and tell him to go away. I would tell him how much I hated him.

It was the only way to get him to leave me alone.

I could see the hurt in his eyes. His face twisted with pain.

I knew he was hurting too and I didn't care.

I just wanted Jacko back … and he was gone, forever.

I wished every day God would've taken me instead.

I hated God.

I hated Liam.

I hated everything.

I spent every bit of nearly eighteen months, in that state of mind.

Even when I came out of the bedroom, where I had spent the first month after Jacko's death, I wasn't truly present.

I was a shell of the person that I was before. I felt dead inside.

My only reason to live and breathe was to take care of Janie. She was the only reason I got up out of the bed and returned to the living world. To care for my daughter.

I was so thankful, she was there.

For Liam, I never returned. I was a ghost in our relationship.

When I finally started to come back to myself, it was too late. Emotionally, Liam was already gone from me. He wouldn't even make eye contact with me anymore.

To make matters worse, he had grown even more cold in the last several weeks. Working late every night on a new project at work.

I knew it was really just an excuse to stay away from home.

Away from me.

I tried to think back to the last time I saw Liam look at me with love in his eyes. Was it before Jacko's death or after? I couldn't remember now.

His touch had long grown cold.

In fact, he avoided touching me at all. There wasn't even a grazing arm, passing in the hallway.

He would go to great lengths to not even be in the same room with me.

Luckily, Janie never noticed the emotional turmoil going on with her mother and father. She was just as joyful, as ever.

Janie was miraculously, a happy, well-adjusted child, despite the tragedy that she had been through. I was in awe of my naturally happy daughter.

What troubled me immensely, was the disconnection with Liam. It was a distinct and cold separation and I had no idea how to fix it.

I had lost Jacko, I wasn't prepared to lose him too.

When the realization hit me, of what was happening between us, I got the idea for the getaway. I needed to get him to really see me and hear me. What I truly needed was to be able to tell him what was in my heart and have him actually listen.

Getting him completely alone was the only way to do that.

I wasn't ready to give up.

Not yet.

CHAPTER 2

W E ARRIVED AT the cabin reservation office just after lunch.

The three and half hour drive up here had been tense, to say the least.

The silence between us wasn't broken up by the chatter of a little voice in the back seat and the usual myriad of questions that preschoolers have about everything. I almost wished I had brought Janie to ease the discomfort.

Now, it was just us, alone, in the truth of the loss of passion, friendship, and possibly … all the love.

The truth was, I did still love him, maybe he loved me too … but it certainly didn't show.

The reservation office was an old, rusty construction trailer on a dirt driveway. It looked as if it might collapse in on itself at any moment. Not too impressive, but this was a primitive vacation after all, so what exactly did I expect?

We walked in and a little bell dinged over the door. The trailer was maybe fifty total square feet and I wondered, did they really need a bell? I almost laughed out loud at the absurdity of it but kept it quiet.

An older guy with a long and completely white beard, sporting a good-sized pot belly, greeted us.

He reminded me of Santa Claus.

"Good day folks, what can I do ya for?" His smile was genuine.

I wished Janie was here to see him.

Santa Claus in his rusted-out trailer.

I almost laughed out loud again.

Liam spoke up, "We have a reservation."

The old man chuckled a little as he looked us over.

"You city folk sure love to play *Grizzly Adams*, don't ya? But you jus' had better be bein' careful. Ain't nobody up there this time a year, so if ya get yerself in some trouble, there ain't goin' be any helpin' ya. You understand?" He posed it more as a statement than a question.

Santa laughed again to himself and shook his head as he filled out our paperwork.

Liam straightened up and stood tall. A mannerism no one would have noticed but me.

"We will be just fine, thank you." His words were sharp as he spoke.

He certainly didn't like his manhood being challenged.

Santa rambled on with some words of advice and then handed Liam a map of the gorge area and the key to the cabin.

"It's 'bout a half's hour drive up there, but ya'll should be in thar plen'y a-fore dark." Santa said as he spit brown liquid into a can.

Liam took the keys, the map, and some other paper-work that Santa handed to him and he walked out without a thank you or waiting for me. I looked back at Santa and smiled weakly. Then, I silently followed Liam out to the car.

The map said it was a fifteen-minute drive to the bridge that went over the gorge and then it would be another twenty to twenty-five minutes after that, up the mountain, to where our cabin was located. It was actually only a few miles up the mountain, but the roads would be treacherous and we would have to take it slow, according to Santa's advice.

The drive up to the bridge was quicker than I expected it to be. There was so much to look at, the time passed quickly. The scenery was lush, even with it being late Fall. The leaves had long fallen from the trees, yet the landscape was still full and vibrant. There were rolling hills, farms, horse pastures, and log cabins with chimneys streaming smoke. We passed a pasture filled with plump, wooly sheep grazing on fall grasses. They lazily lifted their heads to look at us as we passed. Something else I wish Janie could've seen.

We stopped just before reaching the bridge, at a market that looked like it had been there since the 1950's. It had been a full-service gas station in it's heyday. The tall red and white Texaco sign still stood, though the paint was faded and chipped. Rust stains ran down parts of the sign, giving credence to its age. There was an awning that covered a large slab, that had once held a couple gas pumps. They were all but vacant now, except for a few weeds that had triumphantly broken through the oppression of concrete above it. The building looked more like an old house than a store, with its worn wood siding and a rusted screen door that slammed shut no matter how softly you tried to close it.

A brown shaggy dog was laying in the sun, fast asleep near the entrance. Paws twitching, inevitably chasing a squirrel in his dreams. When we opened the door, he lazily lifted his head to get a look at us. His face was graying and his big brown eyes were filled with gentleness. Seeing nothing that interested him, he laid his head back down with a thud.

We stepped inside the market and instantly I wanted to turn around and leave. This was not a place I would've stopped at by choice. It had dusty wood floors and there was an overbearing smell of fried meat and mildew.

I would have turned around and walked right back out but Santa had warned us, it was the last place we'd have to buy supplies. I still needed to pick up some groceries for our trip. I had only brought a few things from home.

This was the only option.

I knew we needed a lot of ice for the perishables because we wouldn't have a refrigerator, so I packed the largest cooler we owned. What I didn't consider was the fact of how much room the ice itself would take up. In all reality, I should've brought a second cooler.

Liam was noticeably irritated by my mistake.

Lucky for me we were able to buy two Styrofoam coolers.

I slowly perused the aisles of the small market with my nose turned up. A *Karen Carpenter* song crackled on the worn overhead speakers, cutting in and out, giving me an eerie feeling. Liam was a few aisles over occupying himself in the hardware section. I figured he was most likely trying to avoid being beside me, rather than actually shopping for anything we needed.

The food selection was poor at best. Most everything was canned, bagged, or dried.

If I had known how much I would long for this market in the near future, I would have shown a little more respect.

I decided on a pack of bagels, cereal, milk, a loaf of wheat bread, a dozen eggs, a bag of pasta and a jar of spaghetti sauce, pressed sandwich turkey, a pack of hot dogs, buns, American cheese slices, a few condiments, cookies, crackers, chips and several other miscellaneous canned goods.

They had a small meat counter, so I grabbed some chicken cutlets that looked as if they had been packaged right there on the property. The thought of it made me shudder a little.

I looked around the shop for a moment in hesitation and wondered if I was buying enough to last for the whole trip. I looked over the items in my basket and counted out the meals. I hoped what I had picked out would be enough to last us the whole time. I was always one to overbuy with groceries, so I threw a few more canned items in the basket. On a last-minute compulsive whim, I grabbed another bag of pasta and finally surrendered.

After all, it was only three days, how much food could we possibly need?

I headed toward the check out in the front of the store and the boards creaked underneath my feet.

On the way toward the counter, I passed by the wine and beer section. They didn't have much of a selection but I grabbed a bottle of red wine, hoping it would help make the mood softer tonight.

As I approached the counter with my haul, a man that looked to be in his mid-thirties, was staring at me, with a smile on his face. As I got closer, I noticed he was missing a few teeth. I tried to not look at his mouth.

"How y'all doin' today?'" he asked, as I hoisted my basket onto the counter.

"Fine, thank you … " I mumbled.

He was wearing a black mesh ballcap that had a deer's head embroidered on it. His button up beige shirt was missing the sleeves and the edges were frayed. He was wearing a thick gold chain around his neck and his blue jeans had black grease stains on them. I wondered when the last time was that he showered.

"Where y'all headed?" he pressed me in the attempt for more conversation.

I didn't answer him because I was stunned, staring at a giant jar filled with a red liquid. There white eggs floating around in it.

The label read: *Pickled Eggs.*

I looked up at the cashier because he had stopped what he was doing and was waiting for me to answer. I knew I couldn't hide my distaste.

"Ummm, we are just passing through.." I lied.

I didn't want to tell him the truth. Just by the looks of him, I was afraid he might follow us up to the cabin. I had watched too much reality TV and it had muddled my reasoning. I didn't know what he was capable of. I didn't want anything to jinx this trip. It was too important.

"Sure hope y'all ain't plannin' on goin' out into the wilderness this time a'year. It ain't safe for ya."

I hadn't fooled him at all.

He lifted his ball cap off his head and scratched his head, then immediately put it back on, never taking his eyes off of me.

I didn't respond, pretending to look at the packaged gum and candies for sale at the counter. He kept ringing up and bagging the groceries while giving me the side eye.

He shook his head. "I don't know what you city folks find so appealin' about goin' up there. More folks get lost up there in them woods, than anywheres else in Nor' Carelina."

I nodded to appease him and then looked out the window at the car.

Liam was already out there, loading our new-found coolers with the ice he had bought.

I paid for the groceries and mumbled a quick thank you, as I headed out to the car to give Liam the cold items. I could feel the man's eyes on me, as the screened door slammed shut.

As soon as I got to the car, Liam rolled his eyes, as he looked at all the bags of groceries.

"Why did you buy all this crap?" His eyes were narrowed.

I shrugged in response.

"Did you get any water?" He scowled at me.

He already knew I hadn't.

I went back inside and bought two, twenty-four packs of bottled water.

Linville Gorge was located on the edge of the southern Appalachian Mountains. Also referred to as the Grand Canyon of the East and hails as one of the most rugged gorges in the United States.

The gorge encompassed twelve thousand acres of wilderness and is part of The Pisgah National Forest, with an elevation average of thirty-four hundred feet. It was one of only two wilderness areas in the southern states.

The terrain was extremely steep and rugged, with numerous rock formations and winding trails through a thick forest of hardwood and pine.

Before the settlers arrived, the native Indians inhabited the gorge and the surrounding areas. They called it "Eseeoh," meaning a river of many cliffs.

It was a beautiful area and despite the dangers, attracted many visitors during the warmer months.

We crossed the narrow bridge that went over the gorge and when I peered over the side, I almost threw up. The gorge was huge. Bigger than I expected it to be. I don't know how travelers crossed it before this bridge was here. It seemed impassible. The rocks were sharp and jagged and the bottom was not visible to the naked eye.

The bridge we were crossing was old and it didn't look like it was in the best condition either. I kept imagining it collapsing and us plunging to our death. I held my breath until we crossed safely to the other side.

As we drove along the curvy road, we didn't see any houses or cars. I began to get nervous about my decision to bring us up here.

It seemed so desolate and empty of human life, yet at the same time, it was the most magical landscape I had ever seen.

In just a few minutes we had made it to Highland Drive and I began to relax a little.

This was the road that would lead us up the mountain to our cabin.

My anxiousness melted away, as the anticipation of arriving at our destination began to build.

As we turned onto the dirt road, we passed by the rental company's other cabins.

A huge sign out front read: *Mountain Vista Cabins*

The cabins were all identical structures and huddled together in a half circle, just like a neighborhood. Each cabin had an a-frame roof line and a small front porch. There was a playground and a large community fire ring in the center. It looked like a fun place to gather.

At this time of year, even they stood vacant.

The rental company only had one cabin for rent at the top of the mountain. I had chosen that one because it was the only one that was truly primitive. The cabins down here still had electricity and some other modern conveniences.

The primitive cabin had been built in the early 1900's by a local man by the name of Daniel Constance and had been obtained in 1995 as a rental property for wannabe survivalists.

It seemed like the ideal choice for us.

The road up the mountain was rough and some parts were rutted out troughs, that shook the car violently.

I was a little worried that our Toyota Camry might actually come apart. This type of drive would probably had been better suited for a larger, four-wheel drive type vehicle.

The road twisted and turned sharply, as we made our way up the mountain. The time dragged on. It was taking much longer than the twenty-five minutes we had been promised.

At many points, I silently questioned whether we were going the right way. There had been several roads that had veered off of this one in different directions. We could have easily missed a turn, but I didn't utter a word.

I wouldn't dare question Liam.

Not now, not on this day.

Even if we got lost, at least we were together, and that was more than I had with Liam in a long while.

The scenery was unbelievable. Rocky mountain walls surrounded us with sudden overlooks into the valley. Even though it was almost winter, it was still awe-inspiring.

I would catch glimpses down over the valley below, here and there as we passed openings, and it would literally take my breath away.

It was almost dreamlike.

Magical.

The hazy view seemed to go on forever, an expansive opening, at seemingly the edge of the universe. Where reality seemed to cease to exist and everything was microsized.

We had the windows rolled down and the fresh mountain air streamed into the car.

The temperature was unseasonably warm for this time of year.

The forecast had said it would be in the high fifties during the day and the low thirties at night.

I had actually hoped for some snow, but so far, the weather wasn't cooperating. I had conjured up a mental image of snow falling outside the window and us cuddled up by a roaring fire.

An ideal I wasn't sure would come to fruition in any aspect.

The drive up was nerve wracking, as we weren't used to navigating rugged mountain roads and we were both growing weary.

The energy was thick in the car. I could sense Liam was regretting coming with me and we hadn't spoken a word to each other during the entire drive.

Suddenly, a large brown deer, with giant antlers, shot out in front of us causing Liam to slam on the brakes. We were thrown into a violent skid and barely missed falling off the side of the cliff.

The terror was so intense that I didn't even scream. I sat with my eyes and mouth wide open.

"Dammit! Where the hell did that come from?" Liam shouted without even looking over at me to see if I was okay.

We sat stunned for a moment, next to the cliff's edge, where we had luckily come to a stop. Another three feet and we would have gone straight over the edge and plummeted down the mountain side.

Liam sat and stared ahead, not saying a word. Then, he slowly straightened out the car and we continued silently up the road.

Not long after, we came upon the street sign that we had been looking for. It looked more handmade, than an official sign, but it was a welcome sight, nonetheless.

It read "Jasper Mountain Road, Private Drive Ahead".

As Liam turned onto the road, my heart raced with anticipation.

This was it.

I had never had to put a lot of effort into our relationship before.

Things had always just worked easily for us.

We just naturally got along.

Even from the very beginning of our relationship, there was a flow to us that many people couldn't understand, and I am sure, they even envied.

I let my eyes close for just a moment, as my mind drifted back to the day when I first met Liam.

I was the shining star of my high school honors program and bound for Yale. I had grown up in Pinehurst, North Carolina and I couldn't wait to leave small town life behind.

It was the summer after graduation and I was reading in the park. I had settled under a tree and just opened *Jane Eyre* to read again. I had read it every summer since I was twelve. When out of nowhere, a football hit me square on the forehead. It startled me so much that I screamed and fell backward onto the ground. As I was sitting back up, I was greeted by a group of cute, young guys who had rushed over to my aid.

They were all apologizing emphatically.

One particular apology caught my attention. It came from a sandy blonde-haired guy with side swept bangs, and the apparent arm behind the football.

He made his way through the group and smiled at me.

"You okay?" His hazel green eyes reflected sincerity. He reached his hand out to pull a piece of grass from my hair.

"I am completely fine!" I laughed, even though my head had started to pound slightly.

"I'm Liam." He smiled again.

I tried not to squint from the pain in my head.

"My name is Juliette Owens."

"Nice to meet you, Juliette Owens." He shaded his eyes from the sun that was now high in the sky.

I looked him over. He was cute. Really cute, in fact. His baby face, broad shoulders and tan skin made him immensely appealing. Once I got my wits about me, I couldn't help but flirt with him. It was something I was quite good at. I knew just the things to say and how to say them.

The rest of the group of boys noticed. They had all been lingering around to see who would be the one to get to talk to me. One by one, they began meandering off, dejected. No dates would come from this disaster, after all. At least, not for them …

I was used to guys biding for my attention, but I never got seriously involved with any of them. I liked to flirt but never took it further than that. I didn't want anything to distract me from my schoolwork. Boyfriends had a tendency to do that. I had seen many of my friend's grades drop off when they were in serious relationships. I wasn't about to take that chance. I had worked too hard to get to where I was at to let anything get in the way.

Even though I was studious, I was far from a nerd. Everyone had always gone on about how pretty I was, since I was a little girl.

Something I took for granted.

I was tall and thin, and my button nose was lightly spotted with freckles. I had long, silky, brown hair that fell lightly around my face giving me an advantage over even the prettiest girls in my school. My round eyes were more sea green than blue and they were accentuated by long black eye lashes. Their unusual coloring always drew attention to me.

Liam took an uninvited seat next to me under the tree, but I didn't mind. The breeze shifted and I caught a whiff of his cologne. The smell gave me a sensation deep in the pit of my belly that I didn't recognize. I could acutely feel the nearness of him and I felt a little woozy. I wasn't sure if it was my head injury or this new rush of emotions that I was feeling … but I was definitely feeling something new, that was for sure. When he turned his head and smiled at me, I knew I was already falling for him.

We saw each other every single day after that meeting in the park, we couldn't see enough of each other. Liam took me everywhere with him. I went with him and his friends fishing and canoeing on the river. We went to the drive-in movies regularly and I was always there to watch their amateur football games. I had never spent this much time recreationally before. My free time prior to this had consisted of only studying and reading. I was enjoying this new way of living. It felt good to be free to do other things.

Liam and I became inseparable and my parents were astonished. When I brought Liam home to meet them, I could tell they were worried about the situation, though they never said a word to me about it. Their faces said it all, so they didn't have to.

That whole summer, I never thought of the future, school, or what my parents thought. I just enjoyed being with Liam and when reality called, I was devastated.

He was headed out to his last year at North Carolina State University and I was off to Yale.

We said our goodbyes and promised to call every day.

I cried … and then I cried some more.

Everyone said I would forget about Liam after I settled into my new life at Yale, but they were wrong. Each day I grew more and more miserable. We talked on the phone almost every night as promised, but it wasn't enough for me. I was confounded. I had never felt like this in all my life. Nothing had ever been more important than school. Not to mention, I had never really needed anyone, or anything before. Yet here I was, desperately lost without Liam and he seemed to be just as miserable as I was.

With all the emotional turmoil going on, I had trouble focusing on my studies. When we got our grades for the semester, I knew I was in trouble. I had never made anything less than an A before and the 3.5 grade average staring up at me from the semester report, was not that.

Christmas break couldn't come fast enough. I had not been able to come home to see Liam on Thanksgiving break because my parents had flown up to Connecticut to spend the holiday with me instead. I secretly knew they were trying to avoid me coming home and seeing Liam. I believed they thought, that in time, the infatuation would pass. What they didn't realize, was that it wasn't infatuation. We were in love and nothing was going to change that.

When the plane hit the ground that December at RDU, Liam was waiting. I pushed past the departing passengers in front of me, ran out and jumped into his arms. We stood in the middle of the terminal kissing, as people passed us by.

I didn't even go home that first night. We rented a motel down on Highway 421 and spent our first night together. We had never made love before. We had made out pretty intensely several times but I never wanted to go all the way. I was waiting for the *right time*.

He had always been very understanding of that and had never pushed the issue.

That night in the hotel, when I initiated it, he was stunned.

"Are you sure this is what you want?" he whispered, his breath increasing.

"Liam, I have never been more sure of anything in my life." I kissed him deeply.

The next morning, when I awoke, he was sitting on the edge of the bed.

"Liam? Are you okay?" My voice was choked with left-over sleep.

He turned and faced me.

"I'm scared Juliette." He looked down, averting my eyes. There was a tone in his voice that I didn't recognize.

My heart and mind began to race. Was he breaking up with me!? Would he really sleep with me and then break up with me the next day!? My parents had warned me about guys like this. Suddenly, I felt like I might vomit.

"Scared of what?" I squeaked out, trying my best to hide my panic and nausea.

He ran his hands through his hair.

"I am standing in your way. You have a bright future ahead of you. Jules, you are one of the smartest people I have ever known, and now because of me you're struggling in school. You worked your whole life to get where you are and now it's all falling apart … because of me."

His voice was soft when he spoke but I heard the determination and strength behind it.

"I love you Juliette, and I would never forgive myself if I ruined your chances for a happy future."

I gasped.

"Happy future!? What kind of happy future would I have without you Liam!? I used to think that school and a career was all I ever wanted for my life but now that I know you, now that I have felt love, I want more." I reached out and put my hand on his arm to reassure him.

He shrugged his shoulders.

"I don't know, I just don't feel right about what's been happening. I mean, don't get me wrong, I want to be with you, more than anything in this world, but I won't sacrifice your well-being for mine. I just won't do it."

He stood up and walked to the window. His back was to me.

I got up from the bed and wrapped the sheet around myself. I walked over and stood behind him with my head resting on his back. I couldn't even remember what it was like to be the me I was before Liam. He was such a natural extension of me now and I was unhappy to see him this miserable with worry.

"Liam, I am not going back."

"Oh my God, what!?" He whipped around with panic in his eyes.

He stepped backwards, several steps away from me.

"I am not going back to Yale." I said defiantly.

"Yes, you are!" he almost shouted.

"No, I'm not. I am transferring to State. I've been thinking about this for a while now. I can be in school anywhere. I don't need a degree from Yale University to be successful. Liam, I want to be where you are. You are worried about me doing well in school? Then let me do what I want!"

He stood and looked at me for a moment. His face was hard and he looked like he wanted to speak up against my idea, but then he softened suddenly.

"Are you sure that's what you want?" he said quietly.

I walked up to him and put my arms around him, as the sheet fell to the floor.

"I have never wanted anything more." I said as he put his mouth on mine.

He picked me up and carried me to the bed. His hands ran over my body and we made love more slowly this time. Not in the same frenzied state that we did the night before. I couldn't help but wonder why I had waited all this time to make love to him.

Before long, I was registered at NC State University and enrolled in the History program. My parents were less than thrilled with my decision, but I didn't care. I was happy. My grades improved and soon I was hailing a 4.0.

Liam graduated in the Spring and got a job working at Cisco Systems in the Research Triangle Park. He was good at his job and he excelled quickly.

We saw each other most nights of the week and I spent every weekend at his place. I was glad to go over there and get away from the dorm life. I didn't fit in with the girls partying and dating lots of different guys. I was an outsider and they couldn't understand why I was so serious about Liam.

Being with him was more of a natural state to me than being alone. As a child I had perfected the art of being alone, lost in my books, but now things were different. Something about Liam completed me in a way I would never understand.

On the second anniversary of the day we met, he proposed. He had taken me to the park and tossed a football in my lap. Taped to the football was a note that read: Will you marry me?

When I looked up from the football, he was down on one knee. He had a hopeful smile on his face.

My heart overflowed with love and excitement.

I was going to be Mrs. Liam Bennett.

I would think back to that very moment over the years. It was permanently etched in my mind and I often wondered lately, if there was ever a way to re-capture the energy of that moment? To bring back the love that was so powerful then?

I didn't know.

I looked over at Liam's face as we turned to drive down the driveway of the rental cabin. His face was stone cold and emotionless, but he was just as handsome as he ever was. His strong jawline hinted a small bit of stubble from not shaving this morning. He no longer had his side swept bangs. His hair was shorter and he now parted his hair neatly to the side for a polished look. Other than that, he looked just as he did the day I met him ten years ago. Not one year showed on his face. I wanted so much to reach out and touch his cheek but I didn't dare for fear of rejection. His eyes were fixed ahead, but I knew he could feel me looking at him. I searched for a spark of that love he used to have for me. I couldn't see it there. Sadly, I could only guess, it had been gone a long while.

All I was left with now, was a small flicker of hope for a miracle.

CHAPTER 3

A S WE PULLED DOWN the long drive, the cabin came into view and instantly my heart dropped.

I couldn't believe what I was seeing.

Rather than the newer, picturesque cabins that we had seen earlier, at the base of the mountain, ours was nothing but a rickety brown shack with a rusted tin roof.

The cabin was built of thin square notched logs with a stone chimney that seemed to lean slightly.

It definitely showed its age.

I involuntarily shuddered. It had looked so much nicer online …

My eyes filled with tears and I tried to swallow them back.

What had I done?

I didn't know if I could even spend one night in this place!

I looked over at Liam. He didn't seem to notice the condition of our rental … or he just didn't care. I couldn't tell which.

As he pulled the car to a stop, I took a deep breath, remembering the reason that I was here.

"*Focus, Juliette, focus.*" I chanted to myself.

It's only three days, and three days could change everything. Little did I know, how right I was about that.

I opened the car door, got out and stretched. The sun still shone brightly. I looked the time on my phone. It was getting close to three o'clock. A strong breeze kicked up and swirled around me, tousling my hair, as fallen leaves rustled in the woods nearby. I took another deep breath, drawing it in slowly and fully. The air was fresh and filled with a smell I didn't recognize, but it was pleasant nonetheless. I looked around. It was beautiful and secluded, just as they had promised. There were mountain peaks off in the distance and the whole property was bordered by deep woods. I couldn't help but warily wonder what type of creatures lurked in those woods. I shuddered again.

I had never been an outdoorsy camping type of girl and I was definitely out of my comfort zone.

Liam opened the trunk and started unloading our grocery bags and luggage onto the driveway.

I suddenly felt very awkward and nervous.

I didn't know how to act around my own husband.

I hesitantly walked over to the car and grabbed some bags from the trunk.

He looked over at me but didn't say anything.

Then, he grabbed our suitcases and headed toward the cabin.

I followed behind him, my feet treading on thick grass, that had already turned slightly golden from the cool Fall nights.

We walked up onto the porch and the boards creaked loudly underneath our feet. The porch ran the span of the front of the cabin. Two weathered wood rockers, grayed with age, sat on each side of the door way. If it hadn't been so worn down, it might have been charming.

Without looking at me, Liam pulled the key out of his pocket and unlocked the cabin door. It squeaked slowly, as it opened. I tried to peer around Liam to catch a glimpse of what we were heading into, but it was dark inside and I couldn't see anything. He walked in first and felt along the wall for a light switch. He couldn't find one.

"No electricity," he said, when he remembered why there wasn't a switch. Then, he chuckled a little, which, I thought was good sign.

I tried to not overanalyze every little thing he did, but I couldn't help myself. I was looking for meaning in everything.

I walked through the cabin door behind Liam, into the darkness. As my eyes adjusted to the lighting, I could see the layout of the cabin. It was an all in one living space. The bed, a small worn couch, sitting chair, and a small dining table with four wooden chairs, were all laid out in the one large room. I walked to the closest window and pulled back the drapes to let some light in, as Liam headed back out to the car for another load. Dust came off the drapes and sprinkled down around me through the sunlight, like raindrops, making me cough a little. As I looked around at our home for the next three days, I felt a sense of peace. It wasn't what I had hoped for but it was okay. That sense of peace lasted until I looked around a little more and realized there was no bathroom. Something I had not thought of when booking this trip. No indoor plumbing. This was literally a primitive cabin, in every sense. I felt a sense of panic rising in my chest and I wondered to myself, exactly how long I could go without peeing.

Liam came in with another load and set the Styrofoam coolers down on the floor in front of me. He was still not making eye contact or conversation.

I dragged the coolers to the wall to get them out of the way. Then, I unloaded the grocery bags, one by one, and placed our items in the small set of open shelves that were arranged over the countertop.

I looked around the miniaturized pseudo kitchen.

There was a stainless sink basin built into the plywood counter but there wasn't a faucet. A large plastic bucket sat next to the basin, which I assumed was for water. On the wall behind the sink, instead of a window, was a small shelf with some dead flowers in a vase and a few paper salt packets. Several tarnished cooking pots hung from underneath it.

Next to the faucet-less sink was a free standing two burner stove top with a cylinder of propane underneath it.

There were also a few cabinets and drawers below the counter and sink, that I didn't dare open for fear of what was hiding inside of them.

I crinkled my nose in disgust at the dirty countertop. There was food imbedded into the grains of unfinished wood.

"Nice. Real nice!" I mumbled under my breath, to ensure that Liam couldn't hear.

I wasn't about to let him hear me complain, after all, this trip was my idea. I honestly didn't know what I was expecting and why I was so shocked at the lack of amenities.

I looked out one of the front windows and saw Liam. He wouldn't have heard my sarcasm, anyway. He was still outside. He had finished unloading and taken a seat on the porch in one of the rickety rockers.

I took inventory of the rest of the space. It was wall to wall wood.

Wood floors, wood walls, wood furniture.

Wood everywhere except the bed and the large stone fireplace.

Not my style, but nonetheless, there was something about this cabin that appealed to me. Something I couldn't quite put my finger on. I hoped that maybe it wouldn't be so bad, after all.

This was my chance to make things right with Liam and that is what I was going to focus on.

Making things right.

I unpacked the bed linens that I had brought with me and walked over to the bed. It was an antique metal bedframe, so far as I could tell. It used to be white, but now was an off color of cream and rust stains. The headboard was ornate with curves and flowers.

An odd choice for this cabin. I opened a window near the head of the bed, to let in some more fresh air. Then, I pulled the dingy, yellowed linens from the bed and held them an arm's reach away from me and tossed them in the corner. I didn't know where else to put them and I had no idea what was living on them.

I honestly, wished I could burn them. That seemed to be the safer choice.

I remade the bed with the comforter and sheets that Liam and I had used when we were first married. A faded floral pattern with blue petals and green leaves scattered all over it. It was soft, worn, and filled with memories. We used this blanket on the bed in our very first apartment. A tiny one-bedroom apartment, whose only view was that of another apartment building's exterior wall. We were desperately happy despite our meager dwelling. I thought of how many times we had made love under these very blankets. How back then, we couldn't get enough of each other. I had secretly hoped that somehow, they still held the magic of the past and they would work to reignite something in Liam again.

As silly as that seemed, I needed all the help I could get.

After I finished making the bed and putting away a few more things, I grabbed two bottles of water and nervously headed out onto the porch to join Liam.

He didn't look up when I came out. He was staring off into the distance. I couldn't read his expression, but that wasn't surprising, as I hadn't been able to in months.

There was a time I could look at him and know exactly what he was thinking.

Now his face, his thoughts, were a mystery to me.

I handed him a bottle of water and sat down in the adjacent rocking chair. We sat together quietly rocking, as a whippoorwill called out in the distance. I could hear insects humming and chirping from the woods and an occasional bird would soar across the sky, just over our heads. I watched as they glided effortlessly through the air.

The sun was still warm and the light breeze that was blowing kept us comfortable.

I was trying to take everything in, happy to just be here with him like this.

We sat that way for a while before Liam got up.

"I'm going to get the lantern going before it gets dark." he announced it so matter of fact, that I had no idea how to respond.

I was frustrated at my loss for words.

I was desperate to make any conversation I could with him and the opportunities were few and far between.

If only I felt comfortable enough to talk to him without any prompting …

I just didn't know how to start.

He went inside briefly and then came back out with a hurricane oil lantern.

After just a few tries, he had it burning brightly. I couldn't help but be impressed.

He smiled to himself with satisfaction. Another good sign.

The temperature began to drop rapidly, as the sun disappeared behind the horizon.

Liam walked over to a stack of logs just to the right of the porch and put his hands on his hips. I knew he had his mind on building a fire.

After a few seconds, he reached down and grabbed several pieces of wood that were already chopped and we headed inside.

I intently watched him bent over at the fireplace. He was working on building the fire. All at once, I was overcome with emotion. How I wished I could just go to him and tell him how I felt. Tell him how sorry I was for pushing him out of my life, especially when he was in pain too. I knew he was trying to help, in the only way he knew how. How I wish I could change everything. Jacko's death … and my behavior afterwards. If only I could turn back the clock, none of this would have ever happened and we'd still have our perfect family. A knot rose up in my throat.

Almost as if he could hear my thoughts, he turned suddenly and looked back at me. There was a softness in his eyes I hadn't seen before but it was gone just as fast as it came, and he turned back to tending the fire.

I had seen it, it was most definitely there, even if it was just for a moment.

I walked over to the fire and put my hand on his back.

"Nice job, honey."

He instantly pulled away from my touch.

His response of "thanks," came out flat and emotionless.

Then, he stood up from the fire and turned and walked out the front door into the darkness.

My eyes followed him out the door but quickly lost sight of him. The sun had well set and without street lights or electricity, it looked like ink out there.

I busied myself in the kitchen preparing a salad from fixings I had brought from home. I chopped up a head of romaine lettuce and then added in grated carrots, baby tomatoes, and cut cucumbers. Then, I topped it with a handful of shredded cheddar. I found a wood bowl in one of the cabinets to put it in and set it on the table.

When Liam finally came back inside, I had him light the stove and I cooked the pasta in a dented blue and white speckled pot I had found in one of the lower cabinets. None of the provisions were nice but they all worked for what we needed.

I set the table with mismatched dishes that had chips all over them, and then I served our meal.

We ate dinner in an uncomfortable silence.

Something we now were used to doing at home. The norm.

I snuck a glance at Liam whenever I could, hoping to make eye contact. He ate his entire meal without looking up.

When dinner was finished, I picked up the dishes and walked to the sink. I sighed audibly. We had forgotten to get the water from outside to wash the dishes with.

"Liam, do you know where the water supply is?" I asked him softly.

"Nope." he answered, as he stood up, his chair making a loud groaning sound as it slid across the floor.

He walked away from the table, stripped down to his boxers and climbed in the bed without offering to go get water or at least help me figure out how to get it myself.

I scraped what I could of the leftovers into a trash bag and tied it up. Then I used a water bottle to rinse off the sauce. I would figure out how to wash them properly in the morning.

I went to my overnight bag and got out a cotton night-gown to put on. I looked around the room nervously realizing there was nowhere to change privately, and I felt a jolt of self-consciousness. Liam was lying on his back looking at the ceiling, so I quickly slipped off my clothes and dropped the nightgown over my head. When I looked back at Liam, I saw that he was watching me. I felt my face redden. As soon as he saw me look at him, he jerked his head away in the other direction.

I slipped into the bed and he turned off the lantern. The fire still blazed and lit up the room with a soft glow. Soon, I heard his breathing getting slower and deeper, he was fast asleep. I lay there wide-awake listening to the crackle of the fire, fighting the terrified thoughts of spiders, snakes, and any other creepy crawly thing that might try to make its way into our bed tonight.

More than that, my thoughts kept going to my husband.

Three days.

Three days was all I had to raise his love from the dead, and so far, I wasn't off to a good start.

After a while of tossing and turning, I finally fell asleep. Sometime in the night, I woke up feeling extremely cold. It was still dark outside ... and in the room. It was pitch black. The glow was gone. The fire had gone out sometime in the night. It was freezing and I could feel Liam shivering next to me in his sleep. I was so cold that even my toes hurt. I involuntarily scooted closer to him for warmth. I was relieved that he didn't pull away, in fact he did the opposite. He scooted over even closer to me. I fell back asleep, smiling, feeling the warmth of his body next to mine.

CHAPTER 4

Liam

I WOKE UP BEFORE dawn and I was in a bad mood. It pulsed through my veins and I couldn't shake it. I was cold and stiff … and I wanted to be anywhere but here. I slipped quietly out of the bed, as to not wake Juliette. I couldn't deal with her looking at me with those doe eyes right now. She had been giving them to me for weeks. She kept looking so innocently at me, like she thought that was supposed to just magically make everything better.

It wouldn't.

In retrospect, I honestly wished she hadn't convinced me to go on this trip. I don't know what I was thinking when I agreed to come. There wasn't one appealing thing about being here, and now the damn fire was out too.

I opened the door of the cabin and walked outside to pee.

No bathrooms … the thought of that irritated me even more.

Another perk of this trip, I thought bitterly.

I could see my breath in the brisk air. I rushed to get back inside, but I didn't know why. It was just as cold inside that god forsaken cabin as it was outside.

When I got back in the cabin, I closed the door quietly and worked on getting the fire going again. I was actually surprised at how quickly I got it going this time. Yesterday, it had taken me a few tries to get it started.

In my defense, I hadn't built a fire since I was kid, living on my grandparent's farm. They had a fireplace in the living room, we used it quite often during the winter, to augment the heat.

I stayed with them a lot as a child because my parents traveled. I was an only child and my parents weren't the 'parents' or 'kids' kind of people.

My father was in a band called 'The Headlocks' and my mother was his permanent groupie. He would play the electric guitar, flipping his long hair around, and she would cheer from the crowd. They spent most of my childhood traveling around with the band, from city to city, looking for their big break. They would sometimes whisk into town to see me, bringing gifts as a substitute for their love and time. Then, without notice, they would be gone again. To Detroit, Philly, LA, anywhere that would pay the band some money to play. The Headlocks never made it big, but still my parents never came for me. They ended up dying in a car accident somewhere in Colorado during a snowstorm when I was ten. My life didn't change much after that, I just kept staying with my grandparents, as I had always done. Then my Grandma died when I was twelve. She was only in her fifties when she had a heart attack, leaving Grandpa and me alone.

Grandpa and I got along great but he wasn't much of a talker, so I spent most of my childhood in silence. I felt isolated from the world, so different from everyone else.

Maybe it was my upbringing, maybe it was genetic, but I never felt like I belonged.

I felt like more of an onlooker, than a participant in life.

That was until I met Juliette. She completed me in ways I didn't even know needed completion. For years, I couldn't believe how lucky I was to have her. She was a shining light in dreary world and she taught me what life was supposed to be like. Full of love and laughter.

That was, until Jacko died. It was just like she died with him.

My bright, beautiful wife was gone and some other woman had taken her place. Her hatred toward me and toward herself seethed into everything … and slowly but surely, my love for her withered away.

I had never held Jacko's death against her.

I knew it was an accident, what happened … but shutting me out the way she did, *that*, I couldn't forgive.

I never thought there would come a day where I wouldn't want to be with Juliette, and now I couldn't imagine staying.

That's why I couldn't figure out what I was doing here in this freezing cabin in the middle of nowhere, with a wife I didn't want.

I had my eye on someone else, anyway.

Her name was Susan.

Susan Landry.

She was an intern at my office. She had long red hair and crystal blue eyes. Long legs. She was sexy. Her smile reminded me of better days and her soft voice soothed my weariness. I knew she liked me too. I could tell by the way she bent over my desk, just enough to where I could see down her blouse. It was enticing. Especially since it had been eighteen months since Juliette and I had sex.

We were talking at the coffee station one day and Susan tilted her head back laughing at something I said. She put her hand on my arm and smiled at me. Right then, something inside of me clicked. I knew I needed to make a new life for myself. Start over again. I knew I would always be there for my little Janie, but I wasn't willing to invest anymore into Juliette. She had used up all of my resources and I wanted out.

It wasn't even necessarily because I wanted to be with Susan, I was just ready to leave. Period.

I had just started talking to a divorce attorney on the day of our anniversary, the day she gave me that damn book.

I sat down in a worn plaid arm chair that matched the style of the rest of the shitty furniture in this place. I tried to be as quiet as I could, because it was sitting in the center of the room, not far from the bed. Of course, everything was within a few steps of each other in here.

"Man, this place is crap!" I thought.

I was actually quite a bit surprised that Juliette hadn't complained once about it. At least, not so far. This was definitely not her cup of tea. Her idea of camping was a ski lodge. A luxury ski lodge, no less.

Despite the environment, I had to admit it felt good to sit here quietly like this. Really good, actually. No phone or TV to distract my thoughts. I hadn't picked up my phone once because I was saving my phone battery, since I couldn't charge it. It was nice to have the restriction and I was surprised how much I didn't miss it.

I couldn't remember the last time I had felt this peaceful.

The fire crackled and I looked over at Juliette, she was still sound asleep. I sat for a while and watched her. Her hand rested across her cheek. I watched the rise and fall of her chest as she slept peacefully. Something she hadn't done since we lost Jacko. I thought of all those nights where she tossed and turned. She cried out his name in her sleep. The pain back then was so sharp. I felt so helpless. She was so sad and there was nothing I could do to fix it. I wished so many times that she would just let me in. Let me try to help her. My gut twisted with the memory.

I got up and poked at the fire to make sure it kept going well. It was already starting to heat the place up. I wanted it to be warm when Juliette woke up.

After all, I was a nice guy.

As I sat back down in the chair, dawn broke and the early morning light poured in through the dingy curtains, spilling onto her face, making her look like an angel. The sight of her took my breath for a moment. She looked so beautiful right then. I had to actively resist the urge to go over to her and kiss her.

I thought about last night watching her change into her nightgown, when I caught a glimpse of her still supple breasts, and electricity spread through me.

I definitely was still attracted to her.

Her body wasn't as fit as it was when we first met but even after having the babies, she still looked good.

Damn good, actually.

These thoughts confused my once firm decision.

She stirred a little and I thought she might wake up. She sighed with her eyes still closed and went right back to sleep.

My heart ached with regret. Why did things have to turn out this way? I couldn't help but wonder, was it really too late? Was my mind really made up?

She stirred again and this time she opened her eyes. She looked over at me and smiled.

"Hi," I said softly.

She seemed startled by my response, then she whispered groggily, "How did you sleep?"

"Okay, I guess. I am sorry about the fire going out in the night."

"No, it's okay Liam, really." She stretched and yawned. "I'll get up soon and make us some coffee and eggs."

I stood up and shook my head.

"No, don't. Why don't you just lie there and take your time waking up. I'll make us some breakfast."

I couldn't believe the sound of my own voice. How could I act like nothing had happened between us, like I wasn't getting ready to leave her?

Somehow, the idea of that seemed further away than it did just a few moments ago.

I fished the egg carton out of the cooler. The eggs were dripping wet. The ice was already starting to melt a little. I highly doubted this stuff would last the full three days. I found a cast iron frying pan that didn't look the cleanest and wiped it out with a paper towel, hoping Juliette didn't notice.

Then, I lit the stove and cracked the eggs into the pan. They made a crisp sizzling sound. A sound that instantly warmed me.

I found another pot to use to make hot water for the instant coffee that Juliette had brought. She knew how much I loved my morning coffee. My heart softened a little more with that thought.

She got up from the bed and came and sat down at the dining table. Her hair was messy from sleeping and she had lines on her face from the pillow, but I couldn't help but think about how pretty she was.

I wanted to stay mad at her, stay firm in my decision, but I could feel my resolve waning more and more.

I set the plate of eggs and a cup of coffee down in front of her and she smiled sweetly. For the last twenty-four hours, she seemed so much like the old Juliette. Even if it was a ploy for my attention, it was nice to be with my wife again.

We sat silently together and ate breakfast.

My emotions were whirling. I was confused and I didn't know how to feel or how to act.

After we finished eating, she got up and took our dishes to the sink. I stared out the window. The sun was all the way up now.

I looked over at my wife and wondered how did we ever get to this place? To where we were virtual strangers. What happened to that young carefree girl that I fell in love with? I watched her as she moved across the kitchen and I realized, even against my own will, I was still in love with her.

Despite all that had happened.

Despite my wanting to go.

I did still love her.

The problem was honestly, deep down inside I knew, I wasn't ready to trust her again.

Not now.

Not yet.

Maybe never.

She could turn again, just as easily, and that's the part that made me angry.

Bitterly angry, in fact.

I could feel that familiar feeling rising up again and I stormed outside.

CHAPTER 5

AFTER BREAKFAST, Liam got up and slammed his chair back under the table and stormed out the door. It startled me so much, I nearly jumped out of my skin. My heart sank. He seemed so sweet, just a few moments ago. It wasn't anything that he said, just something in his eyes that told me that he was coming back to me.

Now without any reason, he seemed angry again.

A few minutes later, he came back inside with a bucket of water. He set it down next to the sink and walked off.

"Thank you." I offered.

He just nodded in response.

I filled the sink with the water from the bucket and began washing the dishes. I didn't find this handwashing soothing. Cold water and no window to look directly out of, made for a dreadful chore.

I also felt myself growing a little resentful at Liam's sudden change of mood. I felt so helpless ... and lost. I didn't know why he was so angry at me when this was both of our faults.

As I finished up the dishes, he came back in, dressed for the day, and quickly disappeared back outside.

He was avoiding me again.

I dressed in a pair of jeans and a plaid button up from J. Crew. I had gone shopping at the mall right before the trip, to buy some things that would work for a cabin vacation. It seemed like something an outdoorsy girl would wear, so I had bought it, along with a few other items that suited the trip. I felt would maybe make Liam see me from a different perspective.

Crazy, I knew, but I was pulling out all the stops.

I tugged on the shirt. I felt uncomfortable in it.

It wasn't my style at all. I usually wore satin blouses with lace trim or soft cashmere sweaters with trousers. My hair, that was still long, was usually worn up in a sophisticated ponytail or a neat bun.

Today I had left it down.

I put my nightgown back in the overnight bag and shoved it past the red lace teddy that I had bought for this trip too. I was having serious doubts about whether it would make it out of the bag. I rolled my eyes at my own naivety of buying it in the first place.

I looked in the mirror at the lines around my eyes. Grief had aged me quite a bit. Next year, I would be thirty and I felt like I was already one hundred years old.

Liam opened the front door and peeked his head inside. "I'm going to go explore for a bit. Be back later."

He didn't give me time to respond and the door had closed before it even registered in my head, that he was going off to explore the area without me.

I almost ran after him, to ask if I could go, but I changed my mind at the last moment and stopped myself in mid-motion.

I stood there and felt like a complete fool. I wasn't going to beg!

My cheeks burned with frustration.

I felt pathetic. Desperate.

I could feel myself getting really angry at his disregard for me. As the anger started to penetrate, I stopped myself.

A new thought had occurred to me.

I began to think maybe it was the best thing for him right now. It would do him some good to go alone.

It would give him to time relax and think.

Think about us ... to think about me.

I felt hopeful as I watched him out the window as he disappeared into the woods.

I walked around our miniature dwelling and tidied up.

Then, I opened all of the windows. The sun had broken the chill from the air and the breeze was refreshing. It seemed to lighten the whole place up.

As I made the bed, I thought about how we had lain close to one another during the night. He had responded to me in a small way. Maybe he was just cold and needed warmth … but now I had even more hope that maybe he wasn't completely gone from me.

Not yet.

He had left a flashlight beside the bed, so I opened the drawer in the night table, to put it inside. Something shimmered in the sunlight, deep inside the drawer. I reached my hand in and pulled it out. It was a necklace. I sat down on the bed and studied it. It was a gold chain with a locket on it. The locket was ornate with carvings and small diamonds on the outside of it. I wondered if the owner of this necklace was also the deciding factor of this bed being in this cabin. I turned it over, and on the back, there was an inscription.

With all my love, James.

I opened the locket and inside was the picture of a baby in a bonnet. A black and white photograph. The picture looked to be the early1900's era.

I wondered about the owner of this necklace. Had she left it here intentionally? Had she suffered a great heartache? Or was it just left here by accident? Something I knew I would probably never know the answer to. I put the necklace back in the drawer and closed it.

I looked at my watch. It was only ten o'clock. I walked outside and squinted in the sunshine. I could hear birds singing in the woods. I sat down on the front step and let the sunshine warm my face. It was surprising to me how cold it was at night and then turn around and be so warm during the day.

After a few minutes of sitting there, I wished I had brought a book to read. I hadn't brought one because I thought I would be spending every moment with Liam. Obviously, that wasn't panning out the way I planned ... and I wasn't used to not having anything to do. Being a mom had kept me so busy during the day, along with the work involved with taking care of the house. I hadn't had time to actually be bored, in years.

I had half a thought of getting Liam's survival book but decided against it. It wasn't exactly my cup of tea.

I got up and looked out over the property. The cabin sat on about three acres of open space. It was bordered on all sides by a dense forest. It seemed almost as if it was a secret haven, but from what I didn't know.

There was a broken down, split rail fence that ran along the perimeter of the property. It ran from the back of the cabin, near the tree line, all the way to the driveway. I walked off the porch and passed the woodpile. Just past it, a faucet stuck out of the ground with a bucket hung on it. I assumed this was where Liam got the water for me this morning. I could only guess it was run from an underground well. The paperwork had clearly stated not to drink this water and I shuddered, wondering what kind of bacteria was in it.

I walked back to the front and saw an inviting opening into the woods.

For some reason, they didn't seem as ominous as they did yesterday.

I stepped onto the path and was instantly enveloped by the forest. The shade of trees made it much darker and I could smell the perfume of the woods. Soil and leaves. I realized that was the smell I didn't recognize in the air yesterday.

The trees gently swayed in the breeze, making a creaking sound while chords of soft light gently filtered down around me. From high up in the trees I could hear the sounds of birds cackling and chirping. I watched as a leaf slowly danced through the air as it fell to the ground.

I was surprised at how pleasant I was finding the woods to be.

I slowly walked the path for a while until I came across an opening to another path that jutted off to the right. On a whim, I decided to go down it.

Within a few minutes, I came upon an expansive mountain meadow under a seemingly endless, crystal-blue sky.

I stood with my eyes wide open, in awe of what was before me.

The meadow was on a gentle slope and interspersed with beech and oak trees. Waves of tall yellow grasses cascaded down the grassy slope. It was sprinkled with colorful fall wildflowers that swayed in the wind.

I walked down the edge of the field running my hand along the top shoots of the meadow grasses and came across a bush of berries.

The emerald green bush was full of round, ripened blueberries.

The unseasonably warm autumn weather must've extended their usual late summer production.

I couldn't believe I had stumbled on these. Liam's favorite dessert was fruit cobbler and I knew these berries would make the perfect cobbler. I couldn't help but think maybe a fresh warm cobbler would soften him a little.

I ran back to the cabin as quickly as I could and grabbed a plastic grocery bag. When I returned to the meadow, I filled the bag with as many blueberries as I could pick. The juice stained my fingers as I picked them, but there was such a joy for me in this simple task.

Once I felt I had picked enough, I headed back to the cabin with my treasure.

I went inside and rinsed the berries with a water bottle and then laid them out to dry on a paper towel. I smiled with pride at my trophies.

The cabin had heated up from the day, so I went over to check the status of the coolers. The ice had melted down quite a bit in the main cooler which made me nervous. I checked the chicken that was in the Styrofoam cooler and it was still pretty cold but I knew I would still need to cook it tonight.

Liam wasn't back yet, so I made myself a sandwich of turkey and cheese. I took my sandwich out and sat on one of the rockers on the porch. Despite the internal stress I was feeling over my relationship with Liam, I felt relaxed. I couldn't remember the last time I felt this good. Sadly, I realized it was before Jacko died.

I thought about his little laugh and his soft, blonde, baby hair blowing in the wind at the park. His blue eyes, that were more sea green than blue, sparkling in the sun. My eyes looking back at me. He was a joyful child and a complete mama's boy. He adored me, almost as much as I adored him. He and Janie were both extremely loving children and they were very bright. They loved me reading books to them and they both were early talkers. They would chatter all day long. They also seemed to have their own language, that I didn't understand. I read that was normal for twins. Even fraternal ones. When they would talk to me or Liam, they wouldn't use that language. They reserved that just for themselves. I always felt a little left out of their circle, but I was grateful that they had each other.

Jacko was the funny one, always making us laugh. I would hear Janie and him talking in the other room and she would be doing that "from the belly" toddler giggle. It seemed somehow, that he just naturally knew what to say or do to make someone laugh.

They were also very creative children, especially Jacko. Right before he died, he had started drawing pictures. He would draw squiggles that only he could recognize as a cow, a dog, or a particular person. He would say "Wook Momma, it you." To me, it was just some lines, but to him it was a beautiful work of art. He couldn't get enough of it. He would sit for a long time with crayons and paper, just drawing away. Which was unusual for a two-year-old. I thought maybe he would grow up to be an artist one day.

Now, he wouldn't be anything.

Except a memory.

My heart ached so much with that thought. I had to fight back the tears. I didn't want Liam to return and find me crying.

To distract myself, I went inside and got the pot that I had washed this morning. I silently prayed that all the germs were off of it. I had no idea what kind of water Liam had brought in to me.

I dumped half of the blueberries into the pot with some bottled water and some sugar. I went to turn on the stove and dismally realized I didn't know how.

I let out an audible huff in frustration. I just left the pot sitting where it was. On a cold burner. I would get Liam to teach me how to light it when he returned.

I went back out on the porch to sit and as soon as I sat down, I saw Liam appear out of the woods. Out of instinct,

I smiled and waved at him. He didn't wave back. I wondered if even saw me.

As he got closer, I noticed he was smiling. More to himself, than to me, but he was smiling. That alone was enough for me.

That was another thing I hadn't seen in a very long time. Liam's smile.

"Did you have fun?" I called out before he made it all the way to the porch.

"It was great being out there. I had forgotten how much I loved being outside in the woods like that."

He sat down in the rocking chair with a thud.

"I'm not used to all that walking though. Guess I am more out of shape than I'd like to admit."

I stood up quickly. "Let me grab you some water."

I ran inside before he could protest.

I brought a water bottle back out to him and he gave me a half smile, opened it and drank the whole thing.

He gave me a half smile! My heart soared. There was really hope, after all! Not wishful thinking … not my imagination … real hope was in that smile.

I went back inside and made Liam a sandwich too. After he ate it, we sat out in the rockers for a while just making small talk. I was beyond thrilled. Small talk was a huge deal for two people who had barely spoken a word to each other in over a year.

We hadn't even fought once during that time. Which I knew was more of a warning sign, than anything else. Two people who didn't care enough to fight were in real danger.

There had been nothing but necessary verbal exchanges between us.

Did you check the mail? Do we need milk from the store? Can you pick up the laundry from the cleaners?

Words that would have been suited for acquaintances, roommates even … just not husband and wife.

So, I was more than satisfied with small talk. Hearing him tell the sights he saw on his outing today was honey to my ears. Telling him about my discovery of berries was a joyful regaling. I remembered this feeling. How it was when we were dating. Hanging on his every word and him listening to me, really listening. I couldn't help but smile.

CHAPTER 6

Liam

M Y MOOD WAS STEADILY declining. I didn't know what she kept smiling about. I was concerned I was sending her the wrong message. Things weren't better between us. It was just talking, nothing more. I thought of all the long talks with Susan and I instantly I had to get up.

I was afraid Juliette would see it in my eyes and know.

I wondered, was talking, cheating?

I hadn't put my hands on Susan, but the thought was there.

Maybe even the desire, but it was more than the physical desire.

It was the long talks with Susan that consumed me.

Susan listened to me.

She laughed at my jokes.

Her eyes sparkled when I entered the room and didn't glaze over in disgust the way Juliette's did.

So yeah, I spent time talking to her. More than I should have.

I knew better. I knew what it could lead to.

I knew it was alienating me even more from my wife, but in my mind, my wife was gone.

That woman I lived with, wasn't her.

It helped me justify my behavior but it didn't really alleviate my guilt.

Not really.

I walked off without saying a word. She was in the middle of talking about the necklace she found today.

Once I thought of Susan, I couldn't keep sitting there.

Who did I think I was betraying? Susan or Juliette?

Really, truth be told, I was betraying myself.

I hated myself for even being attracted to Susan.

I just wanted my wife back, but it was too late for that. She was long gone.

It wasn't as if I didn't try for my marriage. I did try. After Jacko died, I would sit for hours by the bed as she cried. I cried with her. For Jacko, for her. If I tried to reach out and touch her, she would slap my hand away and scream at me to leave her alone.

I brought her flowers every week. Something she adored before the accident. Now, she wouldn't even acknowledge them. Once, she even took them from my hands and put them directly into the garbage can. I never brought flowers again.

Rejection upon rejection, yet I kept trying. Despite the hate and loathing she sent my way. I made dinners, so she didn't have to cook. I did laundry and vacuumed the floors. It seemed the more I did for her, the more she hated me for it. It was like, somehow, she blamed me for Jacko's death.

I mean, for God's sake, it wasn't my fault, it was hers.

I never said it out loud but if she had been watching that day, it would've never happened. … and it wasn't my idea to buy a house with a pool.

I could feel the anger welling up inside of me. I walked out to the wood pile and grabbed the axe. I started chopping wood. Each chop helped me release frustration. I learned this over my childhood. It was my chore to chop all the wood for the winter. Usually after a visit from my parents, I would go chop wood for hours.

After I was finished chopping, I felt a lot more peaceful, more in control.

The frustration and uneasiness would have melted away. In some way, it was a sort of therapy for me.

After I chopped up a few logs, I brought a fresh stack inside and set it down by the fireplace. Juliette was at the stove making something. She didn't even acknowledge that I had come inside.

Irritation clawed its way through me.

I went back out the front door and slammed it behind me.

I didn't know why I was so angry today. I had long passed the point of anger with her. I just ignored her these days. That was how I dealt with everyday life. I treated her like a colleague. Because, basically, that's what she was. A parenting colleague.

Even as I slipped away from her, I expected her to reach out to me. To try to make things right between us. I would've been willing then, to forgive her, if she had just tried to let me back in. To work on our marriage. To be us again, but she never did. Not once did she even smile at me. Not a "thank you" and soon there wasn't even a "fuck you" anymore. We had both grown complacent. They always say, when a couple stops fighting, it's over. I whole heartedly agree with that concept now.

I went to the trunk of the car, pulled out a warm beer and opened it. I had put a six pack in here one day when I had made plans to go fishing last summer. Juliette ended up picking a fight with me and I never went. The beer had been in there all this time. I took a big swig and almost spit it out. Tasted like piss. But piss beer was better than no beer at this point.

I took my beer and sat down in the rocking chair I had adopted since we got here. No sooner did I sit down, Juliette came out.

I was irritated by that, so I got up to walk off.

Before I made it off the porch, she asked, "Liam, could you teach me how to light the stove?"

She didn't make eye contact.

I grudgingly walked inside and showed her how to light the stove. Then, immediately went back outside to my solace ... and my beer. I didn't know what she was doing in there and I didn't care. I just wanted to be left alone.

There was just one tiny problem. The realization I had this morning. It was eating at me. Gnawing at my brain. The fact that I still loved her. It was easy to be mad, easy to flirt with Susan, easy to talk to a divorce attorney, all when you don't love someone anymore. These things become much less easy when you realize you still do love them.

Why the hell do I? That should be the question.

I thought about that morning in the motel so many years ago. After the very first time we made love. She was so adamant about not going back to Yale. She needed me. She wanted me. She was willing to fight for us. Why wasn't she now? Why was she so willing to write me off as a bad investment?

I paused with sudden alarm at my hypocrisy.

Was that what I was doing to her?

I thought about Juliette's face, her eyes, her lips, her body. I was instantly turned on and sickened all at the same time.

How I wished I could just go in there right now and tear her clothes off. Make passionate love to her. Maybe then everything would be okay again. Though, I doubted she'd even respond to me. It had been a long time since I had seen a passionate response from her. After the babies were born, she lost her sex drive. She wasn't the same adventurous girl as before. We made love maybe two to three times a month and I had to beg for it, even then. According to the guys at work, we were doing it more than most married couples. It wasn't enough for me, though. I felt frustrated most of the time. .and after Jacko died, any hope for sex was gone. I think Juliette became a-sexual. I don't know how she could go all this time and not even have missed it at all. I know I did. It was a miracle that I hadn't slept with Susan, who was more than willing to accommodate my needs.

Juliette appeared at the door and I flushed with embarrassment. I felt as though she had intruded on my thoughts and could read my mind.

God forbid, if she did.

"Could you set up the grill? I saw one in the back and we brought charcoal. I have some chicken that needs to be cooked for tonight." she said meekly.

I looked at her in her foreign clothing. Plaid shirt and jeans? She never wore clothes like that … but I liked the way the jeans clung to her. My mind was back on touching her body. I had to physically shake the thoughts away.

I walked around the back of the cabin and found the grill. It was an old rusty *Grillmaster*. I couldn't help but wonder if we could catch tetanus from eating food cooked on it. I dragged it around the front, silently willing it to not come apart during its trek.

I scrubbed the grill top with an equally as rusty scrubber, then I lit the charcoal. The smell was glorious. I wished we had bought some fat, juicy steaks to grill. As the grill heated up, I grabbed another warm beer from the car.

I needed it. Now that I had opened the Pandora's box of thinking about having sex with Juliette, I couldn't stop the thoughts. My body pulsed with the thought of touching her and when she came outside to bring me the chicken, I felt like a savage animal.

I reached out and touched her arm and she jumped back. Instantly, she pulled away, and instantly, the mood was gone. Every sexual impulse left my body and familiar anger took its place.

I practically threw the chicken on the grill and seethed while it cooked.

How dare she pull away from me? She was lucky I was even interested in her. After all she's done! What a bitch!

When the chicken was done, I took it in and threw it down on the table.

She looked at me startled.

"What's wrong?" she asked.

What's wrong? Did she really just ask me, what's wrong!?

"Juliette, really?!" I nearly shouted.

"What Liam?" she asked innocently.

She wasn't going to play innocent with me.

"Why the fuck did you ask me on this trip? What kind of game do you think you're playing?"

She sat quietly for a moment. The longer she was silent, the more enraged I became.

"Juliette, what is wrong with *you*?! I don't even know you anymore! You are a complete stranger to me and honestly, I don't *want* to know you. The *new you*. Whoever, whatever the hell you've become. You can keep it."

I turned and walked out. I slammed the door as hard as I could. Then I punched the outside wall of the cabin. It hurt like hell too. I couldn't help but wonder if I had broken my hand.

She came out after me.

Great, here we go, I thought.

"Liam, please let me talk to you ... " she stammered.

I walked away from her and down the steps of the porch. She followed.

"Liam, please ... "

"What do you want Juliette? I don't want to hear your crap, honestly."

"I need to talk to you." she pleaded.

I backed away from her a few steps more.

"Please ... " she whispered.

I looked at her face expecting to see anger in return for my anger. There was nothing except sadness. I stopped in my tracks. Why wasn't she angry? Why wasn't she lashing out like she used to do?

We sat looking at each other for a long moment.

"Why don't we have dinner and talk over a bottle of wine?" she offered.

"I'm not hungry." I wasn't giving in to her.

"Liam, there are some things I need to say to you and you need to hear them, whether you want to or not. I can tell you are done with me. That's been obvious for a while. That's why I asked you to go on this trip. I wanted to have one last chance to make it right. I know it may be too late, but I want to try. We owe ourselves that."

There were tears in her eyes.

"It's already too late, Juliette." I said it without looking at her. I couldn't bear to see the implications of my words. I turned my back on her. I walked to the car, grabbed a third beer and went to go sit in the woods. I needed to get away from her and fast.

I found a stump to sit on, just at the edge of the woods. I could see Juliette still standing outside, staring in my direction. What did she think I was going to do? Rush back to her side in a sudden change of heart? I don't think so. Sorry lady, that ship has sailed.

Though the honest truth was, I was putting up a good front to myself and Juliette.

Inside, I was dying.

She had tried and I stonewalled her.

I looked at my throbbing hand. It was already turning blue around the knuckles. Not the best idea to hit the wall.

I chugged half of the third beer and felt a little woozy. It had been a long time since I had drunk several beers. They were going straight to my head.

I looked over and Juliette was no longer in view. She must've given up and gone back inside. That was for the best. No need in confusing the situation any further.

I sat there until a chill was in the air. The sun was going down rapidly, as I made my way back to the cabin.

When I walked inside, Juliette was sitting at the table writing something. She didn't look up when I came inside.

I built the evening fire, this time ensuring there was enough wood to get us through the night. Then, I stripped off my clothes and grabbed a washcloth from the bag. I wet the washcloth and wiped my body off. I wasn't used to not showering every day and I felt dirty. After my pseudo bath, I climbed in the bed and stared at the ceiling. Juliette kept writing for a while. I looked at my phone, it was eight o'clock and the battery was at twenty-five percent, even without using it. I was agitated because knew I had no way to charge it without starting the car. Another joy of no electricity.

After a while, she finally slipped into the bed and turned her back toward me. Soon, she was sleeping. I could hear her breathing. Steady and quiet. I stared up watching the shadows and lights from the fire dancing together on the ceiling. I couldn't fall asleep. I had too much on my mind. I tossed and turned and when I looked at my phone again, it was midnight.

I crept out of the bed and went to the table. My stomach growled loudly. I was hungry. On the table was a blueberry cobbler and a letter with my name on it. The cobbler must've been what she was making earlier. I felt a quick pang of guilt. She had boiled the fruit down to a jam, then topped it with crushed cookies. Cobbler was my favorite dessert and she knew that. Another pang went through me. This time it was shame.

I found the grilled chicken in the cooler and put some on a plate and then served myself a large portion of cobbler. I savored every bite. I couldn't believe how good it tasted despite it being made in such a restrictive environment.

I picked up the letter Juliette had written to me. I held it in my hands. I wasn't sure how I felt about opening it. I sat in the firelight holding the letter in my hands. I was skeptical and frustrated. I didn't want to read it, but how could I not? I could just toss it in the fire and never look back. But I couldn't do that, I just couldn't.

I opened it slowly. Her handwriting was beautiful. Slow and deliberate. Each word crafted with care.

Dear Liam,

I wish I had the perfect combination of words to tell you how I feel. Unfortunately, I don't. All I can do is speak from my heart. I want to tell you how I really feel and you have to decide, then, what to do with it. I know you are already standing with one foot out the door. I have felt it for months, but even more so, the last couple of weeks. I have wanted to talk to you, to try to fix what is broken between us, but I couldn't. You wouldn't look at me, you wouldn't talk to me. I had to plan this trip, so I would get the chance to talk to you before you were gone. Now this trip is only one day from being over and I haven't made any ground with you.

I could see by the look in your eyes tonight, that you are done with me. Done with us. Maybe there's no turning back now, but I had to try once more. Since you won't listen to me, I wrote this letter. That way you can read and re-read my words and maybe one day you'll be able to find it in your heart to forgive me.

I know things have been terrible between us. Most of it has been because of me. I did notice that you tried so hard for months to connect with me.

When Jacko died, I wished I was dead instead of him. I felt so worthless, as a mother, as a wife, as a human. It was my fault Jacko was dead and I couldn't do anything to bring him back to us. To give him back to poor Janie. I failed all of us. Seeing your face wretched with agony made it so much worse. I hated myself, I hated us. I wished we had never met. Not because of you, but because of me. I failed in the worst way a mother can fail. I didn't protect my child from harm. I cannot even allow myself to think of that awful day. I can't face it, even now. Just one bit of effort would've saved his life. One thing done differently would have changed the outcome.

I hate myself for that. A day doesn't go by that I don't think about it. That's why I lashed out at you. I couldn't face you and what I had done. I knew if I told you that I hated you, you would leave me alone. The truth is, I never truly hated you. I loved you all along. I longed for your arms to be around me and for you to tell me that everything would be okay. Even though, you wanted to do that for me, I believed that I didn't deserve that comfort. So, I denied you, to deny myself. Denying you became a quick and sure habit. Punishing myself for what I had done. The more I suffered, the better I felt about it. Even Janie couldn't make it okay for me. It was a self-inflicted prison and I wouldn't be set free.

I will be honest, I would've continued on this path if hadn't been for Janie.

I had been reading on some internet posting boards of other women who had lost their children. I kept seeing postings about how women had gotten heavenly signs from their children, that they were okay. One lady had said she had been given a butterfly as her sign and another said a robin came to her. These events had brought them so much peace and closure to have a sign, that their child still existed somewhere in the universe. Rather than be happy for them, I was angry. Bitter that I didn't have a sign from Jacko. Nothing. He was just gone. Like a vapor.

Then one day, Janie and I were at the park. She had climbed up in my lap and I was hugging her. Whispering in her ear, how sorry I was, that Jacko was gone. She giggled and said, "Mommy, don't be silly! Jacko isn't gone. We just can't see him!" She jumped down and ran off to play. Not realizing how profoundly her words had affected me.

I felt that was my sign. The one I had been waiting for. I thought to myself, if she can believe, why can't I? I didn't need a physical sign to believe. I could choose to believe and so I did. That was a few weeks ago. I started to come back from wherever I had been. It was like putting on clothes that are stiff and new. I didn't know how to be me anymore. I had changed. Evolved, maybe. I looked at you and to my horror, I realized you were gone too. The man I cherished and loved, was replaced by a bitter, lonely man. I tried to talk but you weren't interested. You avoided me at all costs. Working late, sleeping on the couch most nights. I couldn't reach you, any more than you could reach me after Jacko's death.

I began to panic. I had lost Jacko and I didn't want to lose you too. That's why I planned this trip. To get you alone, to try to connect with you once again. To bring about a miracle, like Janie did with me that day in the park. Apparently, it is too late for us, but it is not too late for me to say, I'm sorry.

Liam, I'm sorry that I said I hated you. I never did. I'm sorry that I made you believe that I didn't need you. I always have. I'm sorry that I made you feel that I didn't love you or cherish you. I always will.

I am sorry for the additional pain I caused you and for not being there for you when you needed me. I can never take any of my mistakes back. I just hope that I can love you and Janie enough, to one day give back a portion of the love the two of you have given me.

I am also sorry for pulling away from you earlier today, by the grill. I was so startled by your touch. I had waited so long for it and was taken aback when you touched me. I was not rejecting you at all.

You and Janie are all I want in this world.

If you can't be with me now, I understand. I will gracefully back down and set you free.

No matter what, please know, that I will always be there for you, until the day I die.

I love you Liam.

Always Yours,
Juliette

I closed the letter and wiped away the tears that were streaming down my face. I sat quietly for a long while and then, I took the letter and put it in the side pocket of my overnight bag.

I quietly climbed into bed. I still stared up at the dancing lights from the fire. My head swirled with so many feelings. I wanted to wake her up and kiss her all over. Tell her I love her and make love to her for the rest of the night … but I couldn't. I was frozen in place.

I wanted to believe her, but I didn't really. I wanted to touch her, but I couldn't allow myself to. I wanted to forgive her … and move on … but I was still so angry and hurt. My heart wouldn't budge. I wouldn't fall for a trick. I lay awake most of the night and sometime around dawn, I fell asleep.

CHAPTER 7

WHEN I WOKE UP, Liam was sound asleep next to me. I rolled over to check the time on my phone, but my battery was dead.

The early morning sun was peeking through the curtains, so I knew it was after dawn.

I got up and quietly moved across the room.

I went straight to the table to check to see if he had found it.

My letter was gone and there was a dirty plate with cobbler crumbs sitting on there, in its place.

I picked up the plate and put it in the sink, lost in thought.

I wondered what he had thought of the letter.

I wondered if he even read it …

He could've just as easily tossed it in the fire … but … he wouldn't … not Liam.

He would've read it.

I looked over at him, still fast asleep in the bed.

This weekend had certainly proved to be more of a challenge than I expected it to be.

For some reason, I believed that once we were alone together, everything would fall back into place.

He was so angry and still keeping me at arm's length.

He had always been such a kind and loving man before this.

My heart was heavy. I didn't know how I could get through to him. The letter was my last hope.

I knew the pain I caused him must've been great, for him to respond to me the way that he has.

No matter how bad our arguments had ever been in the past, he had never shut me out.

My fear now, was that my attempts to repair the relationship, had arrived too late.

His eyes were empty and his face … so cold.

I thought back to when he found out I was pregnant and how excited and happy he was. Even more so, when he found out it was twins. He couldn't wait to have a family.

Liam babied me the entire time I was pregnant. He showered me with love, massages, and food.

Food was the best gift of all and I couldn't get enough of it. He had even gone numerous times, in the middle of the night, to pick up my random cravings. Fried pickles, mango sherbet, curly fries, cream filled donuts, the list went on. I would be onto another craving before he could get back with the first one ... and for some reason, he still found me attractive. I felt like humpty-dumpty, yet, he never stopped saying how beautiful I was.

I thought he was crazy, but secretly, I loved it.

We still made love several times a week when I was pregnant. For some reason, I couldn't get enough of him, even if I didn't feel very attractive. To Liam, it didn't seem to matter, even when my belly was huge and my breasts were uncomfortably swollen, he still said I was sexy.

My mind drifted back to one hazy afternoon. My belly had just started to swell. We were lying on the bed and he grazed his lips over my belly as he kissed it. That had turned me on so much. I was overwhelmed at the tenderness and love that he had for me.

Unfortunately, after the babies were born, I lost my interest in sex entirely. The doctor assured me that it was normal to feel that way. Fatigue from lack of sleep was the main culprit, he had said.

The problem was, it never came back. I mean, we had our couple of times a month, duty sex, but I just wasn't into it anymore. Not like I used to be. I read online that it would come back in time. New mothers had a tendency to struggle with a nose dive in their sex drives.

Even though we were still making love, my enthusiasm wasn't the best. I felt bad for Liam, but he never complained to me about it. I knew it had to bother him. How could it not?

Then, the accident happened and our sex life was completely over.

Still … he didn't complain.

I was astonished, but I knew in my heart, he was a really good man.

My heart filled with love and gratitude for him. Followed by painful remorse.

I thought of all those long days and nights he stayed beside me, while I lay curled up in the bed, crying.

How he took care of the whole house and Janie, when I wouldn't get out of the bed for that first month.

Even after I was up and functioning on auto pilot, he did so much to try and help alleviate any burdens that were on me.

He tried so hard to bring me back from the darkness.

Showing me love after love, that I never accepted. I gave him only rejection in return.

Now, I just hoped … somehow … I would get another chance with him. To try to begin to pay him back for showing me more love than I had ever known.

These memories made the waiting for him to wake up even harder.

I was consumed … wondering what his thoughts were now. Had it made a difference? Did I get through to him?

I wish I just knew. What did he think of the letter? … but at the same time, I was terrified that I wouldn't like the answer.

I busied myself with some cleaning, to keep my mind occupied while he slept.

First, I wiped down the table and the countertop. Then, I washed the dishes and did some sweeping, as quietly as possible.

I went out onto the porch and swept it as well. It didn't really need it but I needed to keep busy.

I shivered, the morning air was chilly. Definitely chillier than yesterday. I had thought it would be a nice morning to sit out on the porch but I didn't bring a jacket with me. An absent-minded move, on my part.

I went back inside and grabbed an old, red, wool blanket that was laid across the back of the sofa and I wrapped myself up in it. I went back out on the porch and sat in one of the rocking chairs. I chose the one that Liam had been using. I kind of felt like I was stealing it from him. In a way, it was "his" chair.

Which was silly, to feel that way, but it felt like I was taking something that belonged to him. It was a way that I could feel closer to him, sitting in "his" chair.

The porch faced the view of the mountain peaks in the distance. I stared out at them in breathtaking awe. The blanket didn't do much to warm me but I enjoyed being out here, in the serenity of my surroundings. I tried not to think about Liam at all.

I rocked quietly and listened to the sounds of life in the woods. A woodpecker knocking on a tree, an orchestra of birds singing, the breeze rustling through trees, and the early morning crickets chirping happily. The sound was sedating.

I was actually surprised at how much I was enjoying myself.

I had never spent much time in the woods. I never had any interest in it. Not to mention, where I lived growing up, was in the center of town, and the only outside time I spent was walking to the library or reading in the park. My parents were scholars, both holding PhDs. My mother and father both were clinical psychologists and had a joint office in a building downtown. They spent all of their free time reading and learning. There were no televisions in our home. I remember on Saturdays, we would all gather in the living room and everyone would have a book to read. The grandfather clock would tick and we would sit in silence, reading. That was how we spent time together. Family time at its finest. I wondered, if my interest in school was genetic or environmental. I now regretted not spending more time playing as a child, but my parents would not have heard of it. For as long as I could remember, learning was the most important part of living and they made that clear. I was an only child and I am pretty sure I was an accident. Dr. and Dr. Owens did not have time to take away from furthering their education to raise a child. Our home was not a tender place but I knew they loved me, nonetheless. At least, in the best way they knew how. It was strange to me though, how in contrast, I loved being a mother and having a family, so much.

By the time I got back inside, Liam was up. He had made coffee and was sitting at the table shirtless. Seeing him like that, jolted me. His body still looked so good. Naturally thin, he didn't chunk up like a lot of my friend's husbands did. His five o'clock shadow had turned into full stubble. The hair on his face was darker than on his head, giving it the appearance of a full beard. He looked so sexy sitting there.

He didn't look in my direction as I entered.

"Would you like me to make you some breakfast?" I asked tentatively.

"No thanks, I am getting ready to go for a walk." He said without looking up.

My heart dropped. He wasn't going to talk to me about the letter …

All my hopes were falling.

He got up and put on a blue t-shirt and jeans.

"You might want a jacket, it is chilly out there." I offered.

He nodded and grabbed his jacket on the way out the door.

I stood looking at the closed door, fighting back tears. A dark realization was setting in.

He hadn't said a word about the letter …

Maybe he did burn it after all.

I dressed in the same jeans from yesterday and a yellow cable knit sweater. Another find from my shopping trip. I ran a brush through my hair but it was dirty and looked terrible, so I put it in a low ponytail. One thing was for sure, I would be ready for a shower when we got home.

I ate some cold cobbler and then brushed my teeth with the bottled water out on the porch.

When I finished, I went back inside and made the bed.

I sat down in the arm chair by the fireplace and let out an audible sigh. I was lost at what to do next. I had done everything that I could do. The ball was in his court.

I looked over at the darkened fireplace. The fire was out now. Liam wouldn't rebuild it until this evening. I looked forward to that. It was strange how I was getting used to the new routine here.

I just missed Janie so much. I thought of her perfectly round cheeks with one dimple and her laughter … laughter that could light up the world.

I was so thankful that we had not seen any negative effects on her development or well-being from losing Jacko.

Being a twin was a special relationship, one I could never understand. I fully expected her to go through a terrible time after we lost him, but she seemed to take it much better than anyone else did.

Maybe she was made of more grit than I was.

Maybe she understood the workings of the universe better than I did.

I didn't know, but I did know for sure that she was a remarkable child.

They both were.

Suddenly, the door opened and Liam appeared back inside.

"That was quick." I said it more as a question rather than a statement.

He walked over to where I was sitting and stood there like he wanted to say something to me.

"Are you okay?" I asked.

He stood quietly and started to speak and then stopped. He shifted nervously and looked back at the door like he might walk back out.

Then, he turned back to face me.

"You wanna go with me?"

My heart quickened. Did he just say what I thought he said?!

"I would love to." I tried not to sound too enthusiastic, just in case he might decide to withdraw his offer.

"Okay, I'll wait for you outside." He turned and walked out.

Just like that.

I sat in the chair stunned at his offer, for a just a minute, and then jumped up.

He wanted me to go!

I ran over and pulled out a tote bag. I packed it with a couple of waters and the rest of the bread and a few slices of cheese.

The ice had melted in the main cooler and the turkey had gotten warm, so I had tossed it this morning.

I wished I had put it in one of the Styrofoam coolers, though the ice was practically gone in them too. Even the hot dogs and milk were in a questionable condition.

Good thing, it was our last night.

I grabbed the chips and some of the blueberries and threw them in the bag as well and headed for the door.

I stopped just before I walked outside to join Liam and took a deep breath.

CHAPTER 8

Liam

JULIETTE CAME OUT on the porch and she was smiling. My head was reeling. I didn't know why I came back for her. I had planned on spending the day alone again … but I was compulsively drawn back here to get her.

I had made it a few minutes down the trail and images of her were running through my head.

The day we met.

The day we were married.

Her swollen pregnant belly.

Her in the hospital the day after giving birth to the babies.

Her laughter.

Her smile.

I could see her dancing to 80's tunes while making dinner. That was her thing. She called herself the dancing chef.

Happy memories.

I tried my best to shun the images but I couldn't make them stop.

I thought of the words in her letter …

My heart was full, as I thought about her and our life together.

I wasn't ready to jump back into this marriage but I knew I was ready to say maybe.

When I realized that, I wanted to see her immediately.

I practically ran back to the cabin. I couldn't get back there fast enough.

When I got inside, time seemed to stop. I felt so nervous, awkward. Worse than a guy on a first date. I could barely get any words to come out of my mouth. I didn't know what was wrong with me. I almost stuttered. After I asked her to come with me, all I could do was leave as fast as I could. To give me time to regain control of myself.

When she opened the door and came out onto the porch, she was smiling.

Instantly, she took my breath away.

She looked so pretty.

I felt myself smiling like an idiot.

Again, I questioned myself, what was wrong with me? I was acting like a silly school boy.

I took the bag she was holding and we started down the trail.

We walked together, leaves crunching under our feet as the sweet smell of Fall filled our noses.

Neither of us said a word, but the silence was filled with a new energy. I couldn't quite place it, but it felt good.

I felt good. Better than I had in a long time.

I reached over and took her hand in mine and she smiled.

I almost stopped and kissed her right there.

We walked along hand in hand, and I listened to the quiet around us and to the sounds of nature, that I might not have noticed at any other time than this. I took in the soft roar of the wind through the tree tops that stood like mountains over us and the thuds of our feet on the path. The clicking of a cicada in the woods and the intermittent songs of various birds, filled my head like a perfectly timed musical performance.

At that moment, I was in perfect peace.

After a while, we stopped on a small grassy knoll, that was covered in a blanket of sunshine, to eat the food that she had packed. I had to hold back my laugh at our meager lunch. I didn't want her to think I was laughing at her.

As we ate, a squirrel scampered past us. Juliette tried to throw some bread to it but it ran off in terror. She looked so bewildered. She couldn't understand why it didn't want the food.

Sometimes, she seemed so innocent.

We made some small talk about the squirrel; the woods, and how amazing Janie was.

I tried to avoid the topic of anything serious.

I liked being with her like this. It felt right.

The wind blew pieces from her ponytail that fell around her face. She was truly a beautiful woman.

She looked at me and paused.

The expression on her face was serious.

I knew something was coming and I couldn't avoid it.

"I love you Liam. I am sorry for how I have hurt you ... I wish I could take it all back." Her eyes were soft as she spoke.

"I know, I read your letter ... " I tried to deter this conversation.

She looked at me expectantly. She wanted to hear more.

"I love you Jules, more than you can ever know. I am just really mixed up right now. I need you to be patient with me."

I ran my hand through my hair, anxiously.

"I understand. I do. I just wanted you to hear me say it out loud." She reached her hand out and put it on top of mine.

I smiled with relief. She didn't want to hash it out. She was satisfied with what I was able to give her.

This was definitely more like the old Juliette. I knew I had made the right decision to go back and get her.

We cleaned up our lunch mess and started back on the trail. I had followed this trail for a few hours yesterday but had not ventured past this point. I loved exploring and I was pleasantly surprised at how much Juliette was enjoying the hike. She kept smiling and chattering about the plants, trees, and the occasional creatures we would see. My heart continued softening toward her.

We hiked until we reached a river. I grimaced and instantly wished I had brought my fishing rod. The rushing water cascading over rocks made almost a roaring sound. We walked along the riverbank until the waters slowed to a lulling flow. The sunlight reflected off the water, giving it a diamond like sparkle. I instinctively stooped down and picked a few purple wildflowers that I had spotted and handed them to Juliette.

She raised them to her nose and sniffed.

"They're beautiful!" Her eyes sparkled with joy.

My faith in her was growing by the minute.

We walked a little further and then spotted a building that looked like a lodge, off in the distance, tucked up in the woods.

Curiosity, got the best of us and we wandered up to the lodge.

Tall evergreen trees encircled the structure and the ground was covered in moss, giving the appearance of mid-summer.

There were no signs of activity.

The lodge looked like it hadn't been used in many years.

The glass was broken out of one the front window panes and the cedar shake roof looked rough and in disrepair, with loose shingles covering the ground.

The lonely exterior was built of massive logs, now weathered with age, and a deep porch ran all the way across the front. The porch roof was supported by crooked logs made into columns.

On the side of the lodge, there was a tall fieldstone chimney and an old wooden ladder, that was missing several rungs and clearly dry-rotted, leaned up against the wall. It looked as if someone stopped in the middle of a job, and never came back.

There was a woodpile to the right, with weeds growing all through the already chopped wood, and there was a rusted axe laying on the ground.

We walked up on the porch and a blue and grey striped lizard crawled along the railing, unconcerned about our presence there.

Over the front door was a sign that read:

William Semshaw's Fish Camp

Established 1880

Juliette gasped in excitement. This was right up her alley. Living history. I checked the door handle and to my surprise, it was unlocked. When the door swung open, birds scattered and flew up the chimney. Juliette screamed and I laughed out loud.

We stepped inside and the smell of dust and musk met us. It was dark, due to most of the windows being boarded up. Slits of sunlight made its way in through the cracks.

The inside condition was not much better than the outside. The lodge was far from inhabitable.

There were cobwebs in every corner and an inch of dust covered everything. Green vines grew down the walls, making their way from the roof and up through the floor.

Nature was taking back its space.

We walked in further and looked around.

The hardwood flooring was uneven and there was a tattered oriental rug spread across the floor in the center of the room. There was a large fireplace that was surrounded by couches and recliners. They looked as if they were picked straight out of the 1950's. Which, in reality, they probably were. There was a mounted deer head over the fireplace, with strings of webbing dangling from its antlers.

On every wall in the main room, there were dusty, mounted fish of varying sizes. There were also equally as dusty, plaques with the names of the annual fish-off winners from over the years that the lodge was active. The last plaque was dated 1985.

The layout of the lodge was that of a traditional ranch home with a main room in the center. The ceilings were at least fifteen feet high with exposed rafters and beams that spanned the entire length of the room.

There was a rustic looking kitchen off to the right, that looked more like an old tavern than a kitchen. A smoking room was just after that on the opposite end.

On the other side of the room, were the entrances to three bunk rooms. They each had metal bunk beds with tattered mattresses all along the walls. When I opened the door to the third bunkroom and looked in, a snake slithered off into a hole in the floor. I was glad Juliette didn't see that.

I looked around some more and saw that there was no bathroom here, either.

As Juliette wandered off, looking at old photographs, I spotted fishing rods stacked in the corner, and there were lots of them.

"Jules, look!" I called out.

I ran over and picked one up. It was a vintage Garcia Conolon Spinning Rod. It had a little rust on it but still looked usable. I opened the tackle box sitting next to it and sure enough ... weights, lures and hooks.

"Want fish for dinner?" I looked at her and smiled.

She nodded happily and smiled back.

We made our way back down to the river.

The sunshine was warm and just as we sat down on some large rocks nestled along the bank of the river. Just as we did, a nice breeze kicked up.

As I prepped the rod, a bullfrog croaked from an unseen location, then we heard the call of a Spring Peeper, in the distance. I always wondered why they were called Spring Peepers when you could hear them in the Fall too.

I gazed across the river to the other side. There was nothing but forest all around us. It was by far, the most peaceful place I had ever been.

I cast my line into the deepest part of the water.

There was something soothing to my soul about fishing, and the serenity of being on the river always engulfed me.

I spent many of my teenage days on the river.

I hadn't been fishing since before Jacko died and I hadn't really realized how much I had missed it.

Juliette's presence here gave it a warmth that I didn't expect. She hadn't come fishing with me at all, since we were dating. It was nice to be here with her like this. I was in my element and she was willingly beside me.

It gave me a sensation that I hadn't felt in a long time.

Happiness coursed through me giving me a little bit of a high.

Juliette scooted closer and put her head on my shoulder. All was finally beginning to be right in the world again.

CHAPTER 9

W E SAT ON THE ROCKS together, while Liam
fished for our dinner.

I hadn't felt this happy in a very long time.

Finally, he was coming back to me.

We hadn't talked about the letter. He said he needed time
but still …

I could feel him drawing closer with every passing minute.
Something in his mannerism and his smile told me that
everything was going to be okay.

I watched him as he fished. He reeled in several trout and
a bass. He put them on a stringer that he had found in the
lodge. He whistled while he did it.

The sun began to heat us up and he took his shirt off and
handed it to me.

I blushed at the sight of him like that again.

He bent down and adjusted the stringer in the water and I watched as the muscles in his back moved with each tug on the line.

Old feelings were stirring inside of me. Feelings of lust that I hadn't felt in a long time.

It felt good to want him again. To feel like a woman again. I had forgotten how good it felt.

He came and sat down next to me with his rod in hand and I worked to get my mind on something else.

"It feels good to be here with you like this Liam. We should do this more often."

He turned and looked at me, as if he was a little shocked.

"I would like that Jules." He flashed a big smile. I knew I had said something right.

I meant it, too. I never wanted to take the chance of losing him again. We needed time like this together. It was good for us. Good for our marriage.

My family, what was left of it … meant everything to me.

He caught another small bass and I reminded him that it was just the two of us eating and he laughed.

"I thought you were really hungry!" he said jokingly.

I laughed too.

He stood up and let the little guy go back into the river. Then, we went back up to the lodge to return the rods and supplies.

As he wiped down the rod he had borrowed, I walked around and looked at the lodge some more.

In the center of the lodge was a Great Room.

It seemed to be frozen in time. Nothing had probably changed in decades.

Rustic but lovely, in its own way.

In the very center of the Great Room, there was a large chandelier made of antlers. Across the room was the largest fireplace I had ever seen. The inside of it was so big that I could've easily walked inside of it. I imagined it must have been amazing to see when it was lit. Now it was filled with dust and vines.

As I walked along the wall looking at old photographs and plaques, I came across a Victrola windup record player in the far corner. A wooden crate sat on the floor beside it and it was filled with old records. I pulled one out and dusted it off. It was a Louis Armstrong album. The cover was worn and faded but beautiful, all the same. I took it out of its cover and blew on it. I placed it on the turntable. Then I cranked the player and the record started to spin. Soon, the melody crackled out of the old speaker.

Music that hadn't played in many years, filled the room.

"La Vie En Rose" rang through the air.

Liam came up behind me.

"May I have this dance?" he said as he put out his hand.

I smiled as he pulled me close to his body. I felt warm and tingly all over. He placed his hand on the small of my back and we began to sway in unison, as the trumpet blared. The old floor creaked underneath as we turned slowly together. He pulled me even closer and I closed my eyes. I laid my head on his shoulder, as we moved deliberately to the rhythm of the music. He twirled me around and then pulled me back to him.

He put his mouth gently on mine. I kissed him ardently in return. Months of not touching made me feel like a teenager again. I wanted him and he could feel it.

The passion consumed both of us.

He pulled my sweater over my head and I unbuckled my jeans and dropped them to the floor, as the music continued to play. Then I slipped off my panties, as he unclasped my bra. I stood naked in front of him as his eyes burned with desire.

He gently pulled my ponytail out and ran his hands through my hair.

"My God, Jules, you are so beautiful."

I blushed, and then half laughed.

"How can you think I am beautiful? I am a complete mess. I haven't had a shower in days … and I'm not even wearing any makeup."

"Jules, you have never looked more beautiful to me than you do at this very moment." His sincerity was palatable.

He led me over to the worn sofa and stripped off his own clothes. I laid down and he climbed on top of me and began kissing my neck. I put my hands on his well-defined shoulders and pulled him even closer. I wanted him to be inside of me … and now. Eighteen months of abstinence had caught up with me. I didn't want to wait another second.

I was breathless and when he finally entered me, I was consumed by love and blind with lust. I don't think I had ever been so turned on in my life. Each time he moved, I became even more excited. When finally, I cried out as my body exploded with delicious convulsions.

We were both trembling when it was over.

The record was skipping and we hadn't even noticed.

He got up and got dressed and then brought me my clothes. As he handed them to me, he kissed me again.

"I love you, Jules … "

His words were still hanging in the air as I got dressed.

He wandered out of sight, into the kitchen of the lodge. I hadn't been in there yet.

I heard him call out.

"Jules, check out what I just found!"

I followed his voice into the kitchen, if you actually wanted to call it that. It wasn't much more advanced than the one in our cabin, but to my astonishment there were handmade cabinets with intricate carvings and delicate handles.

Exquisite work.

I had to wonder if the same woman who influenced the bed frame in our cabin, had her influence here as well.

There was a long unfinished wood top bar with tall barstools lined up, all the way down it.

Liam stood across the room at the other end of the bar, smiling triumphantly.

He held up an old bottle of liquor.

"Do you think they'd mind if we had a sip?"

"I don't think anyone is going to care, honestly." I laughed.

"It's a Macallan Scotch Whiskey from 1968. Do you know how rare this is?" He was ecstatic and it showed.

I walked around the bar and found a pack of disposable cups in one of the cabinets. I pulled two out and took them to him.

He worked to open the tightly closed lid and when he finally got it open, he let out a shout.

I smiled at him … and this moment.

All I had wished for this weekend, had come true.

He poured us both some in the cups.

He handed me one and then held his cup out to me.

"To us." he said as we clinked our paper cups together.

The taste was smooth and warm. It tickled the back of my throat and I coughed.

We sat together at the bar on old wooden stools and finished our drinks. I wondered how many people had sat in this very spot?

He put the bottle back where he found it and we headed out. Making sure we shut the lodge securely back up.

We walked down to the river and grabbed the stringer of fish, then headed back to the cabin.

We walked hand in hand all the way back in a beautiful silence, both taking in the beauty of what had happened this afternoon.

We arrived back at the cabin a little bit before dusk. I went inside and perused the canned goods I had bought, to find something to eat with the fish, while Liam cleaned and prepped them to be grilled. I was more than happy to miss out on that part.

I found a can of green beans and suddenly realized I didn't buy a can opener. Thankfully, as I searched the drawers, I found one. It looked to be from the 70's but it would work. I also found a couple of emergency candles. I opened the beans and heated them up on the stove, that I was proud to say, I could now light without any trouble. I used the last match from the box we had found in the cabin when we arrived.

I hoped Liam had the ones from the emergency kit that I had given him with his book.

Not long after, Liam called me outside. It had grown chilly again as the evening approached.

"Do you want to eat out here? You can wear my jacket, so you won't be cold." As he spoke, I could see the life in his eyes.

"I think that's a lovely idea." I walked over and kissed his cheek.

I went back inside and grabbed the green beans and the candles that I had found, before heading back out.

"Do you have the matches from your survival kit?" I asked Liam, as I set the plates, beans, and candles down on the old wooden picnic table, that sat adjacent to the house. He had already put the fish out and it looked amazing! I didn't realize how hungry I was until now.

"Yeah, I do, actually!" He ran inside, happy to have a reason to break out the "emergency" kit. I laughed to myself.

He came back and lit the candles, then, took a seat next to me.

I was giddy from happiness.

The trout was grilled to perfection and tasted glorious. I couldn't remember fish ever tasting this good.

As twilight surrounded us, Liam put his arm around me and I sighed.

We sat there together as the sun sank behind the trees. Slowly, the night overtook us and we headed inside.

Liam lit the evening fire as I cleaned up the dinner dishes.

It was bittersweet, the trip was just about over. We would go back home tomorrow morning. I wished we had more time together like this, but I couldn't complain too much. I had accomplished what I set out to do. I had won my husband back. He was mine once more and I would never let him go again.

CHAPTER 10

Liam

I FOUND MYSELF whistling as I built the evening fire. I felt good. Really good, in fact.

I couldn't believe how far we had come in just a few hours.

I stacked the logs in there just right so that the fire blazed brightly and the room began to warm up quickly.

I stood back and admired my handiwork.

I sighed.

I was sure going to miss building fires every night for us.

It was funny, how this primitive life had become so appealing. I felt more connected to myself than I ever had. More like a man. I knew it was cliché to feel that way, but there was something about providing dinner and warmth for my wife that brought out a surge of testosterone in me.

I walked over to where she was doing the dishes with her bucketed water and kissed the back of her neck.

"Do you want me to open that bottle of wine you bought?" I asked.

She nodded and smiled. As I went to get the wine, I suddenly stopped in my tracks.

"Jules, did you happen to see a corkscrew when you were going through the drawers?"

She stopped doing the dishes and looked at me with her mouth open.

"I take that as a no?" I laughed out loud.

I went ahead and dug the bottle of wine out anyway, to see if maybe I could figure out some way to open it.

When I pulled it out, I realized it was a twist off cap.

I laughed heartily.

"What is it?" she looked over nervously.

I could tell she wanted everything to be perfect.

What she didn't realize, is that it already was.

I lifted the bottle high in the air, triumphantly.

"Jules, it's a screw off!"

"I mean, really … what did we expect from a country convenience store wine?!"

We both nearly fell over laughing. I don't know if it was actually that funny or we were just letting off months of tension that had been built up between us.

I poured us both some wine in plastic cups that I found. Surprisingly, it wasn't half bad.

We sat down together on the small sofa in front of the roaring fire. She snuggled up next to me and I put my arm around her.

I felt happier than I had been in a very long time.

We talked for hours about old times and the fun we used to have together. We talked about our first apartment and how tired we were when the babies were newborns.

Somehow, we had forgotten the good parts of our history because we were so consumed with the bad.

That was part of the human condition. Focusing on the negative and letting it blind you to all the good … but tonight … we put all that behind us. We laughed and carried on about how young and naïve we used to be.

We laughed hysterically, about the time we went fishing on old man Eli's pond at midnight that first summer we met. We had snuck onto his property to try to catch some catfish. It was my idea, of course, but Jules was always up for my knuckle brained ideas. We had dragged his old jon boat out to the pond. He had kept it stored next to his barn for years and never used it. We pushed it into the water and climbed in. We drifted out across the water, in the darkness. We whispered and giggled quietly, while I baited my rod. What we didn't realize was the boat had been sitting there beside the barn, because it had a hole. We were in the middle of the pond before we realized what was happening. Water filled up the bottom and quickly covered our feet. Juliette screamed. In her panic, she turned us over. My fishing rods, tackle boxes, everything went to the bottom of the pond, along with the jon boat. We swam back to shore just as old man Eli turned on his porch light. We had a lot of explaining to do to our parents and to old man Eli.

I made jokes and mocked old man Eli's farmer voice, as he yelled and cursed at us.

I tried to be funny, just because I loved to see her smile. It had been so long since she had.

I carried on and she heartily laughed at my wittiness and reenactments of our adventures. It felt good to have her responding to me like this again.

I thought of Susan in the coffee room that day and I shuddered at the thought of it. Guilt pulsed through my body. If I could take back anything I had ever done in my life, that would be it. Letting my affections and interest go toward another woman. Susan couldn't begin to compare to the woman that Juliette was. She never could. I wanted to tell Juliette what had happened, but I was too afraid. I knew she wouldn't understand.

All I wanted right now was to keep things going good between us ... and man, things were good ... better than they had been in a very long time.

I looked at Juliette. She looked so beautiful in the fire-light. The lights danced in her eyes, giving them a sparkle that I had never seen before and I was drawn like a magnet to her. I found myself thinking of this afternoon and how good it felt to make love to her.

At once, I was consumed with passion for her again.

I wanted to make love to her again … right now. Right here on the couch.

I didn't know how she would respond, so I restrained myself and didn't make any moves. I didn't want to push my luck.

Instead, we just kept talking until the fire grew dim.

I added more wood to keep it going, then I went over to my phone that was still on the bedside table, to check the time.

It was completely dead.

I wasn't concerned because I knew I would be able to charge it in the car tomorrow morning on the way home.

It had been nice to have these three days of freedom. Not constrained by the tether of the phone or of time. We had just lived as the moments came and went. In a lot of ways, I was dreading going home. I wished we had a little more time together like this.

Juliette got up and went to the kitchen to grab a bottle of water. I followed behind her. I put my arms around her and pulled her close. My body yearned to make love to her again. I kissed her neck. I felt her go limp and warm under my touch. My heart soared. Her body was responding to me.

I picked her up and carried her to the bed. I tenderly undressed her and then stopped to look at her lying there on the bed. I had to hold myself back, I wanted to jump on her right away, but what I wanted more than that, was to take my time and enjoy touching her. It had been too long since I had really enjoyed my wife.

I laid down next to her and ran my fingertips lightly against her arm and down to her fingers. Her skin felt like silk under my touch. I ran them down her neck, her collarbone, between her breasts, and down her belly. She gasped with pleasure. I enjoyed the power I had over her. Power that was for good. I took my time, watching as her body yearned for more. I loved watching her respond to my touch. As my fingers got lower, she opened her legs for me and I slowly slid them inside of her. She made a moaning sound that turned me on even more. I put my mouth on her soft breasts and suckled them. She put her hands in my hair and lifted my face toward hers and I leaned in and put my tongue in her mouth. The taste of her mouth sent electricity through my entire body. I tried to wait longer, but she pulled my face to her mouth and breathed in my ear.

"I want to feel you inside of me."

I did as she asked. Once inside of her, I moved with slow and steady rhythm until I felt like I would explode and when I heard her cry out in her own release, I let myself go. I moaned involuntarily, as I came inside of her. I collapsed on top of her in a state of euphoria. We laid together quietly. Both covered in sweat. Soon her breathing slowed and I knew she was falling asleep. I rolled off of her and pulled her close to me. I loved the feeling of her in my arms.

I fell asleep that way and slept all night. A deep dreamless sleep.

When I awoke, something wasn't right. It took me a moment to collect my thoughts.

The bed was shaking.

Why *was* the bed shaking?

Then I realized it wasn't just the bed shaking, the whole cabin was shaking.

A picture fell off the wall and the glass smashed on the hardwood floor.

Juliette woke up and screamed. It was an earthquake and it was a big one.

CHAPTER 11

I WOKE UP WITH a jolt, to the sound of breaking glass and the cabin shaking. My thoughts were jumbled and I couldn't make sense of what was happening. I screamed and then I looked at Liam, he was sitting up in the bed. Within a few seconds, the shaking stopped and it was eerily quiet.

Liam looked back at me with wide eyes.

"What was that?" My voice trembled.

"An earthquake, I think. North Carolina has gotten them before, but never one this big … at least none that I am aware of."

He got out of the bed, slipped on his boxers and walked over to look out the window.

The sun was well up but the birds were not singing as they usually did in the mornings.

I was paralyzed with fear. My first thoughts went to Janie. I wondered if the earthquake had hit Raleigh. I picked up my phone and then remembered my battery was dead … I couldn't call and check on her. That thought gave way to panic and I tried to calm myself. I didn't want Liam to see me in hysterics.

I knew my mom would be worried about us as well. She had no idea where we were, I had only told her we would be in a rental cabin in the mountains. I hadn't given her the rental company's number because I knew we would have our cell phones. How I regretted that now. With the phone batteries completely dead, she had no way to get a hold of us.

Liam turned to me, "I'm going to start the car and get my phone charging. I want to check on Janie and your mom."

I let out a sigh of relief. He would call her.

Liam went out to the car and soon I heard the engine running.

He came back inside. "The battery on the phone is too dead to make a call yet. I'll go back in a few minutes to check on it and see if it's charging. In the meantime, I am going to go outside and inspect the place for damage."

I nodded, still in shock.

After he went back outside, I got up and threw on Liam's t-shirt that was on the floor and my jeans. I carefully tip toed around the shattered glass on the floor and picked up the picture that had fallen. Then, I grabbed the broom and swept up all the shards of glass that had exploded everywhere.

As I dumped the broken pieces into the trash bag, Liam came back inside.

"The porch is a little askew and there are some trees down around the property, but other than that, the damage doesn't look too bad here."

He had a look on his face that I had never seen before. Worry, stress, I wasn't sure.

"Did you check the phone?" I asked hopefully.

"Yeah, it is still hasn't turned on yet. Why don't we get everything packed up and get out of here? By the time we are ready to go, it should be charged enough to turn on. I will leave the car running to keep it charging."

I didn't bother to change clothes and quickly threw my hair into a ponytail. I knew I would be able to get a shower soon.

I quickly packed our belongings, while Liam did the last of the dishes and dried and put them away.

I remade the bed with the dingy linens and swept the entire floor.

I wiped down all the surfaces, making sure all in the cabin was as we had found it.

I finished packing up the rest of the food, leaving a few canned items for the next guests.

It took a little more than half an hour to remove all traces of us from the cabin.

As Liam started taking our stuff out to the car, I looked around the cabin for the last time. I sighed, I had actually grown to love this little space.

I followed Liam out and we got in the car. Both of us pretty solemn. I looked out the back window as we drove away, whispering a silent thank you.

The drive down the mountain was a little more precarious this time, due to many fallen trees and branches that were in the road. Liam had to get out several times and pull tree limbs out of the path, so we could continue on our way. This made the drive down take twice as long as it did on the drive up.

While we were driving, Liam's phone finally lit up and turned on.

I picked it up and dialed my mom's number and instantly heard two beeps. I dialed again and I got the same two beeps.

I looked at the screen and saw that there was a message that read:

Call Failed.

I was confused. Why was the call failing?

I tried once more and got the same result.

I was about to try another time and my eyes wandered to the top of the screen. I suddenly realized why the call was failing. I didn't have any signal.

The call would have to wait until we got closer to the main road. I was certain we would pick up signal once we got down there.

We finally made it to the bottom of the mountain.

I looked out the window as we passed by the Mountain Vista Cabins entrance.

I saw that several of the cabins had collapsed. The roof on one of them out front, had completely fallen in. I shuddered, thankful we hadn't stayed here instead.

As we headed toward the bridge, I noticed the damage seemed to be worse down here, than up on the mountain. The stop sign was crooked and there was a carpet of branches and leaves all over the road.

As we got closer to the bridge, I tried the phone again. Still no signal. I was still fidgeting with the phone, when suddenly Liam slammed on the brakes. Our car slid a few feet forward before it stopped completely. In front of us the road came to an end with nothing else ahead, except the opening to the gorge. I gasped out loud.

"Where's the damn bridge?!" Liam shouted.

The tone in his voice made the hair stand up on the back of my neck. Liam never really cursed unless he was extremely stressed out or scared. I think this time, he was both.

He got out of the car and slammed the door … I followed behind him.

We walked to the edge where the bridge used to be and he put his arm out to keep me from getting too close.

We looked down and saw that the bridge had completely collapsed. There were broken pieces of it, scattered all the way down the side of the gorge, as far as the eye could see. We could just make out the other side of the gorge, the entire bridge had come down in the quake.

We stood silently for a moment. Neither of us knowing what to say.

The area was eerily quiet.

No cars, no animal sounds coming from the woods. Just silence.

We headed back to the car and got inside.

We sat quietly together, taking in the gravity of the situation.

Finally, Liam broke the silence.

"Jules, don't worry. It will all be fine. They know we're up here. They'll send help soon."

I nodded, knowing he was right. The worry about Janie's well-being weighed heavily on me. We had no way of knowing how far this earthquake had reached.

He touched my hand. "And don't worry, I am sure Janie is fine too. These kinds of quakes are usually localized."

How did he know just the right thing to say?

He put his hand around my neck and pulled me close. He kissed the top of my head and held me there for just a moment. Then, he backed the car up and turned around to head back up to our cabin. Or so I thought.

I was surprised when he turned into the cabin neighborhood instead.

"I think we should check it out. They have electricity, you know." I thought I almost saw a smile.

"And a bathroom facility … " I added with a small laugh.

We pulled in and as we got closer, I realized the destruction was worse than I had previously thought.

All of the cabins had sustained some kind of damage and were uninhabitable.

We got out and walked toward the cabins, to get a closer look.

Suddenly, the ground began to shake underneath our feet again.

I ran to Liam and he held me tight.

"It's just an aftershock. It's okay."

His words brought little comfort. I was terrified. There was something that was so unnatural about the ground moving underneath of you.

The shaking only lasted a few seconds and it was over. Suddenly, we heard a crashing sound in the distance, as another of the cabins completely collapsed. They had been built inexpensively and weren't meant to withstand this type of force.

Liam looked at me and half laughed.

"Looks like we are going back to the primitive life."

I didn't mind that fact so much.

Another day up there with Liam wouldn't be so bad.

We talked on the drive back up, like we were just out for a Sunday drive. I think we were both trying to remain positive and not let worry get the best of us. After all, there was absolutely nothing to worry about. They'd have rescue crews coming for us.

Most likely, they would arrive before the afternoon was even over.

Liam had to stop a few more times on the way back up, because more limbs had fallen in the road from the aftershock. Our little car seemed to struggle more this time, as it fought its way up the steep incline. The pitted road caused it to shake us even more than the earthquake had. It seemed it might come apart at any moment. About two thirds of the way up, the car sputtered and lurched forward. It sputtered again and then came to a complete stop.

I looked over at Liam and he put his head down on the steering wheel.

"What is it?" I asked.

"We are out of gas." He spoke just above a whisper.

"How is that possible?" My mind whirled with confusion.

"We had just at a third of a tank of gas when we left the registration office. The old guy said it was a half hour's drive to the cabin. I figured we had plenty to make it up there and back. But the drive took so much longer than we expected both times and now we were going back up again. Not to mention we left the car running while it charged the phone too."

He hit the steering wheel in frustration.

"Dammit!" he shouted.

"I should have known better than to risk this."

I reached out and put my hand on his arm.

"It's okay, Liam. Don't worry. We aren't too far from the cabin." I smiled at him assuredly.

He got out and pushed the car to the shoulder of the road. It still stuck out in the path of any passing traffic, because the road was so narrow, but at least he got it somewhat out of the way.

Truth be told, without the bridge, there wouldn't be any cars coming down this road any time soon, so it really didn't matter either way.

We were certain the rescuers would come in a helicopter. They had no other way across the gorge.

We took what we could carry and headed back to the cabin on foot.

Liam was completely silent. I could feel the frustration seething off of him. I tried to make small talk but he wasn't in the mood. After a while, we both grew tired under our load, so we stopped for a break.

Liam sat down on the side of the road and stared off in the distance.

I looked at my husband. He looked worn. Somehow, he aged in just three days.

I went and sat down next to him.

"Hey, I'm not worried about any of this. After all, if I have to be stranded in the mountains with anyone, who could I have chosen to be here with, that would have been better than you?" I smiled and tapped his ribs playfully with my elbow.

He looked at me and smiled back. That had done the trick. The stress seemed to melt right off of him.

After a few minutes, we started back up to the cabin and it wasn't too long until we saw the sign for Jasper Mountain Road.

We both smiled.

"Home sweet home!" Liam laughed.

We made it back to the cabin and I suggested we leave everything out on the porch. Feeling certain the rescuers would arrive this afternoon.

Liam agreed.

We sat outside on the rockers all day, talking and laughing, while we snacked on leftover cookies and chips.

Waiting.

When the light grew softer and the air got chillier, we knew they wouldn't be coming today. We moved everything back inside and Liam made a fire.

I fished the bottle of wine out of my bag that we hadn't finished the night before and poured us both a glass of it.

We sat together quietly in front of the fire, until we both grew sleepy. I made the bed again with our bedding from home. Then, we snuggled in and fell asleep.

Morning dawned in what seemed like an instant and I could hear birds singing outside of the window. I couldn't remember the last time I had slept so deeply. I rolled over with sleepy eyes and saw that Liam was not in the bed. I got up and stood by the fire that was still going. The air in the cabin had a slight chill to it.

Liam was not inside the cabin, so I grabbed the red blanket from the back of the couch and wrapped up in it for warmth.

I walked out onto the porch where I found him sitting in his favorite rocking chair. He was sipping a coffee.

"Hi there, sleepyhead! I didn't think you were ever going to get up." He joked.

His face was bright and full of optimism. Gone was the look of worry and concern of yesterday.

The air was cold. Much colder than any of the other mornings we had spent here.

I went over and sat down in his lap to get warm. He wrapped his arms around me.

"Any sign of anything?" I asked.

"Nope, nothing yet, and I think I am going to head to the car here in a little bit and get the water that we left behind."

I turned around and looked at him.

"Do you think we are going to be here a while?"

"No, not at all, but we need to have water either way. Even if it is just one or two days."

I leaned back against him. He was right. We had chosen to bring other things with us when we left the car yesterday. The bedding, the remnant of food and our clothes were taken. We had chosen to leave most of the water behind, aside from a few bottles, due to the weight.

"Well, if you're going … then I'm coming with you." I said assertively.

He laughed and his eyes twinkled.

"Well then, if you insist." He squeezed me tighter.

After a while, I stood up and went back inside to get dressed. I put on a pair of khaki shorts and the plaid button up. I couldn't handle wearing the dirty jeans for another day. I knew it would be still a little chilly early on in the morning but it would warm up as the day wore on. Then, I tried to run a brush through my dirty hair. A ponytail was in order again, as my hair was reaching the maximum point of dirtiness.

After I was dressed, I went into our bags to see what I could scrounge up for us to eat for breakfast. The perishables were all trashed yesterday before we had left, including the eggs, and we had finished all but three pieces of the bread.

I took the remnant of the leftover blueberry cobbler and warmed it in a pot and spread it across some crackers.

We ate our pseudo breakfast together, appreciating every bite. We were starving. Chips and cookies didn't make much of a meal for us yesterday, especially considering that's all we had eaten the entire day.

After our breakfast was finished, Liam looked at me and smiled.

"You ready for our adventure?"

I nodded happily.

I grabbed my tote and brought it with me, just in case I found anything else in the car I wanted to bring back.

I walked outside to join Liam, who was already out there, waiting for me. He smiled at me as soon as I came out onto the porch.

Despite the circumstances being what they were, I couldn't help but feeling desperately happy, as we walked down the gravel road together, hand in hand.

CHAPTER 12

Liam

T HE WALK TO THE CAR was pleasant. The temperature warmed up as we walked and Juliette babbled on about getting home to see Janie and the upcoming holidays.

I hadn't seen her this happy in a long time and it was good to see her this way.

She went on about Thanksgiving and what she wanted to cook. She talked about taking Janie to the annual Christmas parade and to see Santa.

It made the time pass quickly.

It also helped that the walk back down to the car was much easier than the walk up, due to the fact that it was all downhill. Plus, we weren't carrying a load.

I knew what was coming though and I dreaded it. The walk back with the water would be a challenge, but I also knew it was a necessity. We would need to bring them all back with us.

I didn't tell Juliette this fact but I knew we had no guarantees on when the rescuers would be coming.

Especially, if they were stretched thin with the after effects of the disaster.

When we made it to the car, I pulled the water bottles out of the trunk. There were less here than I remembered. We had just one pack of twenty-four left, plus maybe a few more loose bottles back at the cabin. I didn't know exactly how many, but I knew there weren't a lot.

I wondered how we had gone through that much water in just three days?

Water preservation had not been on the forefront of our minds ... and why would it have been?

It was definitely on my mind now.

"Do we need anything else?" I called out to Juliette.

She couldn't hear me. She was digging around in the backseat.

She emerged smiling.

"What did you get?" I asked.

"Granola bars and gummy worms!" She laughed.

"I keep them in the car for emergency snacks for Janie ... and well ... uh ... me." She looked at me sheepishly.

I laughed. She was so damn cute.

"You need anything from the trunk?" I asked again, now that she could hear me.

She peered inside and crinkled her nose at the garbage bag full of the trash, from our weekend, that I put in there yesterday when we were leaving.

"I don't think so … " she said as she shook her head.

I grabbed an extra flashlight from the glovebox and a few napkins. I also found an old analog watch that was surprisingly still working. I handed them to Juliette and she put them in her bag.

I locked up the car and we started back.

The sun warmed us up a little as we walked back to the cabin. With only one pack of waters to carry, it wasn't as treacherous as I had imagined.

We didn't talk much on the way back. We were just taking in the scenery and enjoying being together. We had not had this sense of easiness between us in a very long time. Despite the situation being what it is was, I felt satisfied and almost a little glad we would be stuck up here a little longer. I would be fine with a few more days like the one we had yesterday. That was for sure. I looked over at Juliette and smiled. She looked back at me with a return grin.

As we were walking along, we suddenly heard a noise coming from the woods just to our right.

Juliette stopped and looked at me wide-eyed.

"Liam … what's that?"

It sounded big whatever it was.

"Probably just a deer." I assured her, not entirely convinced myself.

We stood watching the woods for just a moment and the sound grew louder … and closer.

Suddenly, a dark shape came into view and there was no denying what it was.

A large black bear was headed straight toward us. He didn't seem to be in a hurry but he was definitely headed our way.

Juliette screamed. I dropped the waters and covered her mouth.

"Quiet Jules! Listen to me. Don't scream!" I raised my voice and then lowered it again and whispered into her ear.

"I read in the survival book you gave me, about bear encounters. They said black bears usually only attack if they have young nearby or feel threatened. In that case, the best thing to do is to lie perfectly still and play dead. Don't worry though, they said those cases are few and far between. This one is probably just curious. He will probably just check us out and then he will move on."

As I spoke to her, the bear came completely in sight. I felt Juliette trembling but she didn't scream. I felt fear pulsing through me, as well. It was less than fifty feet away now.

The bear was solid black with a tan snout and was breathing loudly. Its shaggy fur glimmered in the sunlight, that filtered in through the trees. Funny, how something so dangerous, could look so innocent. The bear stopped and looked directly at us, as if it was just as surprised to see us, as we were to see it. Then, it stood up on its back legs and sniffed the air. It was a huge black bear. I guessed it was probably seven feet tall when it stood all the way up. It looked at us for a few long seconds and then dropped back to the ground. Slowly it turned and meandered in the other direction. When it was out of sight, Juliette collapsed in my arms crying.

I held her close and stroked her hair.

"Shhhh … he's gone now. We're safe." I reassured her, but even as I said it, I could feel my hands trembling.

I steadied myself, trying to keep calm. If Juliette had known how afraid I had been, she would have lost it.

After Juliette regained her composure, we finished the rest of the trek back to the cabin.

I sat on the porch while Juliette made us some lunch, thinking about the bear encounter. I was ashamed at my unpreparedness for a situation like that. Movies and books paled in comparison to real life experience.

Soon, she came out with a warm bowl of baked beans for each us.

"The general store haul?" I asked.

She nodded. "Yeah, we have several cans of baked beans, tuna fish, and a few veggies left."

"Good thing you got all that stuff Jules. Thank you." I smiled warmly at my wife as a pang of guilt went through me about how I treated her that day at the store.

The rest of the afternoon, we sat on the front porch and watched for our rescuers to arrive.

Waiting.

When dusk came, we gave up and went inside.

I made the nightly fire while Jules made us tuna fish and crackers for dinner. We ate by candlelight. Jules laughed and talked to me while we ate, as a sense of uneasiness began to settle in my bones. Something didn't feel right about this situation. I wondered when the rescuers were going to come. It had been two days already.

The next morning, I suggested we go for a walk to break up the monotony of waiting. We left a note on the door for the rescue team and headed into the woods. It might not have been the best idea, but neither of us could stomach sitting on the porch waiting another full day.

We took one of the paths that veered further up the mountain through a forest of mixed hemlocks and tall white pines, swaying in the wind, with a thick undergrowth of rhodo-dendron, mountain laurel, and greenbrier.

We climbed higher and higher until we reached an overlook. The valley below was expansive and we could see the river snaking its way down below us. The rolling foothills were covered with evergreens that stood tall and proud. It was the most beautiful thing I had ever seen.

There was something healing being out in nature like this.

I think Juliette could feel it too.

We sat down on a large boulder and looked at out the view.

Juliette snuggled up against me and started kissing my neck. Her breath was heavy as she ran her tongue up my neck and behind my ear.

She stood up and began taking her clothes off. One piece at a time. She looked at me with electricity in her eyes. Once she had everything off, she stood completely naked in front of me. This view of her body was much better than the one I had been looking at and just as exhilarating. I took my jacket off and laid it down on the rock. I pulled her down next to me and she laid down. I slipped off my pants and got on top of her. We made love with the vista as the backdrop. I had never felt so much ecstasy in all my life.

Afterwards we lay on the rock looking up at the sky. Juliette lay in the crook of my arm and fell asleep. I could have fallen asleep myself but I knew we would need couldn't risk it. We would need to make our way back soon. I let her sleep for about twenty minutes before waking her up, so we could get going.

We stopped by the lodge on the way back.

Juliette went to the kitchen and found some rice and a bag of flour. She triumphantly brought a few canned goods and set them on the table in the main room. I picked up one of the cans and looked at the label. It had expired in 1990.

"We can't eat these Jules. Put them back. We don't need to be getting food poisoning out here."

"What's wrong with them?" She semi-whined.

"They've been expired for 25 years!" I laughed.

She huffed and took the cans back to the kitchen.

I searched through a cabinet in the main room and found a pack of playing cards, more candles, and a few newspapers to read. It might be interesting to see what was in the news so long ago. The papers were dated 1988. Confirming this cabin had been vacant for a long time.

Before we left, I made a silent promise to find the owner of the lodge and repay them for all we had taken. Just as soon as we got home.

That night we feasted on rice and cheese, made from a powder packet of cheese we found at the lodge.

In my mind, it was in questionable condition but Jules swore it was fine to eat.

I put on a Bob Seger album from a playlist on my phone. I knew it would run the battery down, but I justified it, knowing we didn't have cell service anyway. I figured we might as well enjoy some music.

We sat there together eating, like we didn't have a care in the world ... but deep inside of me there was a gnawing fear starting to grow. Another day had passed since the quake and the rescuers still hadn't come.

Water and food was running low. We were living on borrowed time.

Morning dawned dark and when I awoke, I could hear rain beating on the tin roof.

Juliette stretched and yawned. "What time is it?"

I picked up the watch and checked.

"It's eight thirty." I answered.

"Oh good, I can still sleep in some more!" she said triumphantly.

I laughed inside. I couldn't help but wonder, what pressing thing was she avoiding getting up for?

I looked at my beautiful wife as she pulled the covers back up around her face. She peeked out with just her eyes, half closed.

My heart overflowed with gratitude.

I was so thankful to have my wife back.

My dear sweet Juliette.

I couldn't believe how close we had come to divorce.

What was lost, was found again. Everything was perfect. Well, almost …

I had been struggling the last couple of days about whether to tell her about Susan. It felt wrong to hide it from her. I wanted to clear the air. Give us both a full fresh start. I just had to find the right time to tell her.

I got up and stoked the fire, and then went to the kitchen to search through the food we had left for something to make for breakfast.

I found the flour that Jules had brought from the lodge and some baking powder in the cabinet. I mixed them together with a little sugar and made some pretty pathetic pancakes. I also made a syrup from sugar and a little water.

Jules was so surprised and happy over my gesture that she didn't complain once about the flavor. I know they were awful because I had trouble choking them down myself, but they were food and we couldn't afford to be picky.

The rain was still pouring and when we tried to go sit on the porch, it was too cold to stay out there. So, we came back inside.

We needed something to do and I had a pretty good idea of something we could do.

I looked at Juliette and was instantly filled with lust. I didn't know how I had survived as long as I did, without sex.

"I have an idea of something we can do … " I stepped toward her.

"Oh really?" she laughed and I could tell by the look in her eyes, she knew what I meant.

"You will have to catch me first." She laughed again.

I stepped closer and she darted away. I lunged and almost grabbed her but I missed as she screamed and laughed hysterically.

We went around the bed, the couch and I almost had her in my grips when she slipped away again and ran out the front door into the pouring rain.

I called out, "So that's how you want to play?"

She screamed again, as I darted out the door after her. We ran in circles until I finally caught her. She was drenched. Rain ran down her hair and face. Tiny droplets caught on her eye lashes. She was so beautiful. She was wearing one of my white undershirts and nothing else. I could see her nipples through the wet shirt and my body instantly ached to put my hands all over her.

I pulled her close to me and put my mouth on hers. She responded with her tongue darting in and out of my mouth. My body was on fire. She put her hands in my hair and pushed her body against mine, kissing me deeper. Then she took my hand and led me back into the cabin. Our feet made wet footprints that led to the bed.

I stripped off my clothes and then lifted the wet t-shirt off of her. We laid down on the bed together and began kissing again. She pushed her body against mine and kissed me ardently, grinding against my leg. Then she straddled on top of me and moaned softly as I entered her. I ran my hands up and down her body and onto her breasts. Her nipples were erect and her eyes were glazed with passion. She tilted her head backwards and moved her hips slowly at first, almost like she was dancing. Then she leaned forward and moved faster and faster on top of me. She moaned louder and just when I didn't think I could hold back anymore, we both came and she collapsed on top of me.

I thought again how easily I could get used to this way of living. I loved how the simple life suited us.

If we just had food, water, and our sweet Janie.

Juliette got up from the bed and walked over to the kitchen to get a bottle of water. She was still naked. The sight of her made me want to make love to her again, right then, but I restrained myself. I felt like an animal.

She climbed back onto the bed and gave me a sip of the water.

"I could get used to this life." I told her.

"Yeah, me too." she said in a sultry tone that came across almost as a purr.

She laid down next to me in the crook of my arm. I couldn't believe how lucky I was. Truly, I was the luckiest man alive.

Almost as if it was an omen, the rain stopped and the sun came out.

Later that afternoon, after we had played a few rounds of rummy with the cards I had brought from the lodge, I looked over at Juliette, who was tidying up in the kitchen.

I decided it was time to tell her everything that I had been holding back.

I needed to tell her about Susan. I had to get it off my chest.

Juliette needed to know my heart and where I had come back from. I knew it was a risk but I wouldn't be at peace until the truth had come out. She had been so sweet and understanding the last few days. So much so, that I felt I could trust her with the truth.

"Jules, I need to talk to you."

She stopped what she was doing and looked at me. She could tell by the tone of my voice, it was serious.

She walked over and sat down next to me on the couch.

"First of all, I want you to know how happy I have been the last few days. I cannot remember ever being this happy and I am so thankful we have been able to re-connect the way we have."

I paused, as I watched her face go from concern to relief.

"There is something I need to tell you though … "

The panic returned to her face almost immediately. I put my hand on hers to reassure her.

"The morning before you gave me the book … I went to see a divorce lawyer. I didn't proceed with the paperwork though, because there was something in your eyes that day. Something that made me pause. I had to see what would happen if I went on this trip with you … and now I am so thankful I did."

I touched her face with my fingertips, letting them glide down her cheek.

"I am so thankful too, Liam." Her eyes sparkled when she spoke. "You have no idea how happy this all has made me. I never want anything to separate us again."

"Jules … there's one more thing … "

I paused because I knew this would sting.

She smiled waiting for what I had to say. She had no idea at what was coming next.

"There was somebody else … "

Her face turned white and she slid back from me.

"Somebody else?" there was a slight shriek to her voice.

"Her name was Susan. She works with me. I didn't sleep with her … but we had a relationship. A friendship, of sorts. The reason I am telling you about her, is because … well … I wanted to sleep with her. The feelings were there and that's what scared me the most."

I paused again.

Juliette's face was twisted and her eyes turned red.

"Jules, I didn't love her … I was just confused. You left me completely alone and I was lost without you." I stammered, already wishing I could take the words back.

"You didn't love her?" she questioned, not seeming to have heard anything else I had said.

"No, not at all! I was just lonely. She was somebody to talk to. Deep inside, I still wanted you. She was just a band aid on a deep festering wound. A wound that only you could heal. She could never be you and I know that now. The only woman for me is you Jules. Just you and only you. I knew this would hurt you but I wanted you to know about her because I never want to keep anything from you. I didn't want anything hanging over us and I can't forgive myself, until I know you can forgive me. It was wrong and I'm sorry. I really am."

At first, I thought it would be okay. She didn't flinch or fly into hysterics, she just sat staring at me as tears streamed down her face. I reached out to touch her and she jerked away.

I tried to continue to explain. I wanted to be able to say something to her, something comforting, something to ease her mind about Susan but the words wouldn't come.

She didn't say anything, she just stood up and turned her back to me.

"Jules?"

When she turned around to face me, the look on her face made the hair on the back of my neck prickle.

Regret seeped through my bones. I knew right then, I shouldn't have told her.

"How could you?!" The veins in her neck bulged.

"How could you Liam?!"

I started to speak and she ran to me and pounded on my chest. I grabbed her arms and pulled her back.

"Juliette! STOP IT NOW!"

She didn't stop.

"I hate you! How could you do this to me? I was hurting and you went to another woman?! FUCK YOU, LIAM!"

She ripped out of my grasp and stepped backwards. She stared at me with disgust in her eyes.

I felt the rage building inside of me. I trusted her with the truth and this how she responded?!

"Juliette, this is EXACTLY the behavior that caused this situation in the first place! You just don't get it, do you?! You don't understand me at all and you haven't in a long time. You don't care to either. You only care about what you are feeling! How *you* hurt. How *you* lost a child. How *you* were alone. What about ME? I hurt. I was alone. I lost a child too, you know. You are so selfish Juliette. I am trying to make things right and all you want to do is feel sorry for yourself!"

"I have a right to feel sorry for myself Liam!" she screamed.

I didn't listen. I walked back toward the couch, I wasn't going to listen to her excuses. I refused.

She followed closely on my heels and before she could say another word ... I spoke.

My heart had instantly grown cold.

"Juliette, I don't want to hear it from you. You have nothing to say that I am remotely interested in hearing. I am done with you! You hear me? I am done!"

The words were still ringing in the air when I heard the front door of the cabin slam shut.

I turned around and she was gone. I knew I should go after her, but I didn't.

I didn't want to.

She destroyed everything that we had just re-built in just a few seconds time.

I *was* done.

Really done this time.

CHAPTER 13

I RAN OUT THE DOOR of the cabin, blinded by my tears and anger. I ran into the woods and down the trail. I didn't stop until I reached the meadow.

Once I reached the opening, I was finally able to calm myself. I walked along the edge of the meadow until I reached the place where the blueberries were. The bush was mostly bare now. The cold had taken its toll on them.

I sat down on a patch of grass nearby. It was damp from the rain earlier. It soaked my shorts immediately and gave me a slight chill, but I didn't care. Soon, the afternoon sun shone down and warmed me back up.

I drew my knees to my chest and rocked back and forth.

I was still crying, as Liam's words were running through my mind, on repeat.

"Her name was Susan … I wanted to sleep with her."

He wanted to sleep with her *and* he had a relationship with her!? He was lonely!? How could he even think of another woman, with what I was going through!? My heart ached with the betraying words.

"How could he?!" I cried out into the meadow.

At first, I seethed with anger. Angry tears fell down my face, but soon I felt the seething turn to a deep sadness, as memories from the past came into my mind.

I thought about the look on his face, all those times I told him how I much I hated him, after Jacko's death.

When I pushed him away from me.

When I told him to go away and that I wished he would disappear.

How I wished we had never met.

How he disgusted me.

I did it for months as he tried to pull me close, to help me, to soothe me. I purposely hurt him over and over again.

I heard a small rustling nearby and a brown bunny hopped across the edge of the meadow. I watched it as it nibbled on something in the grass. I found myself staring absent-mindedly at it, as the daylight grew softer and the sun began its descent. The sight of the furry little bunny, would have normally had me squealing with delight, but it didn't this time. I barely recognized its presence here.

My thoughts were still with Liam.

I rolled his words around in my mind and suddenly a feeling of deep compassion and sympathy washed over me. He was right. I knew I had not given a lot of thought to what he was feeling. I was focused on myself and my own pain. I took for granted that he was okay. I justified it with that he seemed to be okay. Now I wondered, how much of that okay-ness was put on for my sake?

I thought of his words in the cabin, just now. He *had* been sad and alone. He had lost a child too. He had seemed so strong though … I really didn't know how much he was hurting … at least I pretended not to know.

I had hurt him so deeply with my rejection.

The reality was, he needed me just as much as I needed him.

He had tried and I didn't.

… and he didn't sleep with her. Even though he wanted to … he didn't.

He chose me. He chose us.

Right then, I knew I needed to let this go and forgive him for what happened. I had to make this right, somehow. If it wasn't too late. I felt ashamed at my outburst. He had trusted me with something that made him completely vulnerable to me and I lashed out at him rather than truly listen to what he was saying. I had worked so hard to win his trust back. His love back. Then, I responded in the same manner I had before. With hate and anger.

It hurt that he was involved with another woman, yes, but I loved Liam and he loved me and that was really the only thing that mattered.

I left the meadow, just as the sun began to set. By the time I made it back to the cabin, it was almost completely dark outside.

The cabin wasn't lit up. There wasn't the usual glow from the fire or from the lantern. I opened the door quietly.

"Liam?"

He didn't answer me.

"Liam?" I said it a little louder this time.

He still didn't answer.

Then, I saw his silhouette as he sat in the arm chair, in the dark.

As I got closer, I could see he had been crying.

The sight of that nearly paralyzed me. My heart ached with regret.

"Liam, I'm so sorry … What you told me … it was just too much for me to process.

When I thought of you with another woman, it made me crazy with jealousy … but I understand now.

At least, I understand why it happened.

I don't like it, but I understand ... and I am so sorry ... so very sorry for leaving you alone the way I did. You were right. I didn't think of your feelings at all and I will always regret that. You were hurting and I shut you out. I am sorry for that and I am sorry that I wasn't more understanding when you bared the truth to me earlier. I wish I would have responded differently ... "

He didn't move or respond. He just stared off into the darkness.

"Liam?"

He made no move to respond. I could see it was of no use to try.

"If you want me to leave you alone ... I will." I said quietly. I felt defeated inside.

He had said he was done and he meant it.

As I turned to walk away, he reached out and grabbed my hand.

"Don't go ... " His voice was barely above a whisper.

He pulled me down into his lap and hugged me. Tighter than I think he had ever hugged me before.

We sat like that in the darkness for a while before he spoke.

"I'm sorry too Jules, I never meant to hurt you." His voice was just above a whisper.

He leaned back so he could look into my eyes.

"You didn't deserve that and it was selfish of me. I should have just kept trying for us."

I pulled him close to me again. "Shhhh, it's okay. We were both in a bad place. What's important is that we are okay now." I meant every word.

We sat that way holding each other, until Liam got up to make the nightly fire.

Three more days passed as we settled into a routine of waiting, trying to ignore how dire our situation was.

On day 7, we woke up solemn. We were down to our last few bottles of waters. Despite how careful we were being, we were almost out of everything. We had been eating fish that Liam caught every day and that had kept us going. We knew it wasn't enough to sustain us long term and now the water was almost gone.

We also had to finally face the fact that no one was coming for us.

Somehow, we had been forgotten.

I sat out on the porch while Liam cut firewood for the evening fire. When he was finished, he came up on the porch and sat with me.

We sat quietly, neither knowing what to say.

"We only have enough water to last us a few more days." His voice had a strange tone to it.

"We will die within a few days without water, Jules. We could try to boil the water from the faucet, but I am not entirely convinced it would be safe to drink, even then. Getting dysentery out here would definitely be a death sentence."

I just nodded in response. There was a lump in my throat that I tried to swallow back. Crying wasn't going to help this situation and I didn't want to add more pressure on Liam, with him thinking I was falling apart.

"I am going to have to go get help." He said it so assuredly, I knew he had been thinking about it all day.

"You can't cross that gorge, Liam," my voice just above a whisper.

"I don't have a choice. If I stay, we will both die. It is the only chance we have."

I sat quietly trying to digest the thought of him crossing that gorge. When I was researching the cabin and the area around it. I had read the stories about people who had been lost or died in the gorge and those stories were of people who were seasoned hikers. Liam had never hiked seriously or mountain climbed before … and even with experience that crossing would be treacherous. They said a mile on Linville Gorge does not equal a mile anywhere else. It was known for the most unapologetically rugged terrain in all of North Carolina and it was so easy to get lost because most of the area was unmarked.

I shuddered at the thought of him trying to do this alone. It absolutely terrified me.

"I'm going with you." I said assertively.

"No, you're not." His voice was flat.

"Yes, I am Liam. You're not going alone." I crossed my arms in defiance.

He looked at me without saying a word. Then, he got up and walked out in the yard to gather up the wood that he had chopped for the fire.

I made the last can of beans to go with the fish. I had been saving these to ration out, but we would need the extra nutrition to gain our strength for tomorrow.

"Oh wow, we are feasting tonight! A whole half a can of beans!" Liam laughed as he sat down at the table. I couldn't help but laugh too.

We ate, while Liam carefully examined the map and various other paperwork about the State Park, that Santa had given us.

His forehead was crinkled up as he studied it. His face showed the beginnings of a full beard now. He put his hand on his chin and rubbed the hair on it while he was lost in thought. His knuckles still bore the scabs of where he had hit the wall in anger, just over a week ago. I couldn't help but think about how handsome he was.

After a while, he leaned back in his chair and put his arms behind his head as he spoke.

"It is a nine mile walk to the gorge from here, then I am guessing it will be a two to three hour climb down to the river basin followed by a three to four hour climb up the canyon wall.

According to what I am reading, anyway.

"It shouldn't be too bad ... hopefully." he said more to himself than me.

We crawled into bed later, not saying much to each other. We laid together in the darkness, neither of us could fall asleep. The reality of what lie ahead, was hanging over us. It loomed, like a darkened cloud that threatened to burst into a violent rainstorm.

Fear crept through every cell of my body. I knew how dangerous the gorge was. I realized we had just as much of a chance of dying out there, as we had from dying here, without water. I wondered if Liam was as aware of the dangers of the gorge, as I was?

I wondered if he was afraid?

I could feel my own panic rising up and fought against it to keep from screaming out in the night.

I didn't dare utter a word out loud, I knew if I did, I would lose control. Thoughts ran wildly through my head, as I desperately tried to ignore them. I laid like that until the wee hours of the morning when I finally fell into a restless sleep.

When dawn broke, I sat straight up in bed. Liam wasn't there. I jumped up and ran to the door. As I went to open the door, I heard chopping.

Why was he chopping wood when we were leaving this morning?

I opened the door and looked out at him. I immediately wished he wasn't exerting all that energy. He need to save it for the climbing.

"Liam?" I called out from the porch.

He didn't answer or look up.

I went back inside, deciding to let him be. He probably just wanted to replenish the wood for the next set of guests. We had used all the stores up. Though with the bridge out, it would most likely be a long time before anyone rented this place again.

I packed Liam's bag with four of the six waters that we had left and put the other two in my bag. Then, I packed his bag with the last three granola bars, along with the emergency kit from his book, and the flashlight from the car.

In my bag, I put the red blanket and the first aid kit. I planned to pay the rental company for it because I didn't have a jacket with me and I would need it for warmth.

I looked around the cabin, trying to think if there was anything else we needed to take with us. I realized I shouldn't pack much or add to the weight we were already carrying. That would only make the trek harder. So, it was down to necessities only.

By the time Liam came in with an armful of wood, I was ready to go.

He put the wood down next to the fireplace.

"Do you remember how to start the fire?" he asked.

"Yes ... " I said hesitantly. He had taught me last night, I thought he was teaching me just for fun.

"Don't go outside after dark, and I would rather you not go into the woods at all."

My brain reeled. What was he saying?

"I shouldn't be gone more than a day."

"What do you mean?" I was confused.

"I am actually thinking it will be a quicker hike than what I thought. It should only be just around ten hours or so before I reach the general store. I may even luck out and run into someone on the road before then. At a minimum I could stop at a house, if I see one, and use their phone."

"Hell, I could be back here before nightfall." He half laughed.

"Liam, what are you talking about? I am going with you."

"No, you are not. You are staying here and I will be back with help soon. This is not negotiable Juliette."

"Liam, I *am* going." I felt the edge in my voice.

His face was expressionless.

"Let's get something straight Juliette, you are not going. You hear me?" His tone was harsh.

"YES, I AM!" I shrieked.

He took two steps toward me, his faced twisted with anger and frustration.

"DAMMIT, YOU ARE NOT GOING! Do you understand me!?"

I stepped back, startled by his anger.

His face immediately softened a little.

"Look Jules, I'm sorry. I don't want to yell at you. I am just scared. I have to get us help. This is the only way to get us out of here. Please try to understand that I am doing what's best for both of us. It is going to be hard enough to make that crossing on my own, without worrying about looking out for your safety too."

He looked so worn with worry and fatigue. I wondered if he had even slept at all last night.

"I want to be there to help you … " My voice cracked.

"If you really want to help me, then stay here."

Everything inside of me wanted to protest. To yell, to argue, but I knew by the look on his face that he meant what he said. I wasn't going to make our last few minutes together, a big fight.

He came up to me and held me tight. I couldn't help but cry and then the tears turned into full out sobs.

"Please don't leave me Liam." I cried.

"I have to Jules. Please don't make this harder on me, than it has to be."

I was numb, as he walked over, picked up his bag, and inspected it. Then he added a few more items to it and removed two of the waters.

"Keep these here." he commanded.

"You'll need more than two waters." I insisted.

"No, it is only a few hours. I will be to civilization by nightfall. I want you to have these just in case there's a delay in getting transportation out here. I can't imagine it will be more than twenty-four hours. But don't worry, I really think I will be back before sundown."

While he was busy checking on the fire, I put the other two waters back in his bag. Luckily, he didn't notice or he would have protested.

He put on his jacket and a baseball cap. Then, he threw the bag over his shoulder.

I walked with him out to the edge of the property. He turned around and hugged me tight.

"I love you Jules. Please don't ever doubt that. No matter what has ever happened between us. I have never stopped loving you. When we get back home, I am going to do everything within my power to make sure you and Janie have the happiest lives that anyone could ever have."

"Liam, we already do … "

He leaned over and kissed me.

He started to walk away and I grabbed his arm.

"It will be fine, Jules. Trust me. I will be back before you know it!"

He smiled at me and started down the drive.

He turned back just before he disappeared around the bend, waved one last time, and called out, "See you tonight, beautiful!"

As he disappeared out of sight, I had to fight every urge to run after him.

He was gone.

I stood there looking at the place where I saw him last, and I began to realize how alone I really was. Truly alone. Something I had not ever experienced, in a real sense. I had always been with someone, my parents, my roommates in college, then Liam. Someone had always been there. I felt sadness … and then I felt fear. I looked around at the forest around me and felt a cold chill run down my spine.

I instantly hoped he was right about being back fast and that it wouldn't take a full day for him to get back to me.

I prayed with every ounce of my being, that somehow, someway, he'd back tonight. Even though I realized the improbability of it, I held onto that hope.

I stood there for what seemed like an eternity.

I looked one last time down the drive after him and then turned and made my way slowly back to the cabin.

CHAPTER 14

Liam

THE FIRST PART OF THE walk wasn't so bad. It was all downhill and it actually seemed I got down to the car faster than we did when we came to get the water.

I tapped it on the hood, as I passed by it, as if to say hello. My backpack was light and I was making great time. I had a good feeling about the plan that I had made. A day's walk ahead of me, at the most. I hated leaving Juliette behind but I knew it wouldn't be for long. Besides, I had no choice. I wasn't going to sit there while we both died from lack of water, waiting for help that was never going to come. Seven days had passed and there had been no sign of a rescue.

What had to be done, had become an obvious fact.

It was up to me to save us.

The trees made a canopy overhead and shaded the road. The air was colder than it had been before and I wished that I had a little sunlight to warm me. Even with walking, I wasn't heating up much.

In the back of my mind, thoughts nagged at me about the chance that I could be outside overnight. If I didn't make it all the way across the gorge before nightfall, sleeping out in the elements would be a certain fact. I would never get through the gorge in the dark. I was going to be lucky to cross it safely in the daylight.

I worried about the cold and hypothermia. If it was this cold now, what would it be after sundown? I pushed the thoughts out of my head and kept moving.

After a few hours, I stopped for a break and sat on log that jutted out with a strip of warm sunshine resting on it.

I pulled out one of the water bottles Juliette had packed for me and took a small sip. I knew not to drink too much at once. I needed to conserve what I had the best I could.

I was feeling pretty fatigued already.

I hadn't slept much last night, because I was too stressed to fall asleep and even after I did, I tossed and turned until just before dawn.

I certainly felt the effects of that now.

I wondered about Juliette and what she was doing without me there.

I hoped she had listened to me and stayed in the cabin. I missed her. I wanted nothing more, than to bring her along, but I knew all too well the dangers of Linville Gorge. I couldn't look after myself and keep her safe at the same time. It was too risky. I had to stay focused.

After a few minutes of rest, I got up and started walking again. I couldn't afford to sit here any longer. I was tired. More than I should've been. I vowed to myself that I would get in shape, when I got back home.

As I walked, it felt like I was moving in slow motion as I passed naked oaks and elms that lined the road. I wondered what time it was. I had meant to grab my watch but had forgotten it.

It felt like this road was going on forever. I had no concept of the distance I had covered.

Miles of trees beside me and the dirt road in front, all ran together.

To occupy myself, I filled my head with thoughts of Juliette. I was so happy to have her back. It was something I never thought could ever happen.

I remembered sitting in a stiff black leather chair at the divorce lawyer's office as he asked me about property division and custody. I looked around his office at the formal furniture and dark green curtains. He had plaques, awards, and framed artwork of ducks and marshes hanging on the walls. He was completely bald except for a few strands of hair that he swept over the top of his head, in a meager attempt to retain the appearance of hair. He wore a three-piece navy-blue suit and green and yellow striped tie and always spoke with a serious tone and a sophisticated southern drawl. When he asked me about alimony and child support, I wasn't shaken at all.

I wondered to myself, why talking about these things didn't upset me.

My heart was so cold and the will to leave her, so strong, that those topics seemed natural and in order.

Being away from her was my one desire then, and now all I can think about was getting back to her. So strange how the tides could turn.

When I finally made it to where the cabin neighborhood was neatly nestled in the woods, I shouted for joy. It was a small triumph, that felt huge.

I stopped and rewarded myself with half of a granola bar and a few more sips of water before I started my descent down into the gorge.

The gorge loomed ahead of me as I stood at the edge of the precipice and looked down.

My stomach dropped with dread.

It really did seem impassible.

I had no ropes; no poles and I wore nothing but tennis shoes on my feet.

Not to mention, I had no real experience with wilderness hiking. I had always dreamed of doing a wilderness trek one day but I had never gotten around to it.

Even though I had been obsessed with watching the survival showmen on reality TV, it in no way prepared me for what I was about to do.

I had read the tales of the perils of hiking in Linville Gorge and these stories were from experienced hikers with supplies.

I had only a prayer and the will to survive to help me.

I started down the edge of the gorge wall and lost my grip almost immediately on some loose rocks, slipping and falling down about ten feet into a tree. I was bruised and got a pretty good scratch on my arm. Luckily, nothing worse had happened.

I re-steadied myself and started back down the decline. The path was treacherous as I slipped and slid down through low lying limbs, clinging to them, as I passed. There were many rock outcroppings that I had to climb over and places where the brush had overgrown the ledge, giving the appearance of solid ground, when in actuality, there wasn't anything underneath, except for open air. If I had stepped into it, I would have fallen to my death.

The terrain was extremely rugged, beyond anything I could have imagined. Each step I took felt treacherous. Life threatening.

The sun was getting lower in the sky and I knew I only had a few hours left until sundown. I realized it was inevitable that I wouldn't make it to help before dark. I just prayed I wouldn't have to spend the night on the gorge wall.

I slipped numerous times, banging myself up pretty good on brush and rocks. My feet and knees were starting to ache but I knew there was no turning back now. I blocked out the pain and pushed through.

I climbed down, what had to be seventy-foot inclines, as my hands slipped and searched for places to hold onto. I didn't think, I just moved. Slowly and assuredly.

The climb down was incredibly steep and rocky but I finally got to the bottom of the gorge wall and breathed a sigh of relief. I was sore and bruised, but none worse for the wear. I felt triumphant. Now, I could sleep on solid ground tonight.

I barely noticed the temperature drop as I walked into the basin. I was beginning phase two of my journey. I hadn't made it as far as I had hoped but I had a sense of accomplishment. I had successfully descended the gorge wall despite the odds against me. I knew now with confidence I could make the incline back up the other side tomorrow. It may be more strenuous but hopefully safer. I knew I should be back with Juliette by tomorrow afternoon and the thought of that kept my spirits up.

I could hear the sound of the river rushing and got to it just as the sun set. The colors were glorious, reflecting on the river. It was a spectacular sight.

I sat down on a large, smooth boulder that jutted out into the water and rested. I ate the other half of the granola bar from earlier and took a few more sips of water as the day turned to complete darkness.

After I finished eating, I laid down on the rock, using my backpack as a pillow.

I looked up at the night sky and it was riddled with stars. There was a countless number of them, just above me. Billions of years old, twinkling in the night.

I saw a shooting star dart across the sky, trailing a stream of light.

As I watched for more to appear, my eyes grew heavier and soon I was asleep.

I slept restlessly and woke up shivering just before sunrise. It was chilly next to the river but I had fared well. I was pretty stiff and it took me several minutes of moving around to loosen back up.

There was a mist over the river and the birds were beginning to sing their morning jubilee.

I looked as the early morning sun's rays reflected neatly across the water.

It was truly a beautiful morning.

I could see the enticement of the men that leave and go on thousand-mile treks alone in the wilderness. I had never felt so alive and refreshed despite my second lackluster night of sleep.

From the other side of the river, I heard the sound of rustling leaves coming from the woods. The sounds grew louder and closer by the minute. I was frozen with fear, as I thought of the bear that Juliette and I had seen. My heart was clenched in my chest when suddenly three deer burst out into the clearing. I almost laughed at myself for being so irrational but kept quiet, as to not startle them.

They cautiously walked toward the water's edge. Their heads darting around nervously. When they decided it was safe, they all three drank from the river. I stood in awe at their beauty and grace.

After the deer had disappeared back into the forest, I began searching for a safe place to cross the river. I had hoped to find a path of rocks to walk across but I couldn't find anything like that. It looked as if I would have to get in the water to cross. I looked for a shallow spot and every-where I looked the water was high and fast flowing.

I was discouraged but continued the search.

I followed along-side the river for a while with leaves crunching under my feet and wildlife flitting in and out of view. They were all busy with their morning duties. I saw birds, squirrels and I even saw a beaver who was completely unimpressed by presence here.

I walked along until I finally found a place that I felt I could safely cross. The water was still rushing but not nearly as fast as it was, further back up river.

I slipped into water that immediately came up to my chest. I lifted my backpack over my head and moved toward the other side. The ice-cold water immediately made me numb, taking my breath. The rocks were slimy underneath my feet and the flow was faster than I expected it to be. I nearly slipped under the water several times but managed to keep my balance and finally climbed up the other side of the bank. I was soaked and freezing cold. I took off my shirt and pants and wrung them out to remove as much excess water as I could. It was difficult to get them back on but I managed it. I was shivering and it felt like the temperature outside had dropped. I couldn't be sure if it was because I was wet and cold or if it was actually getting colder.

After I was dressed again, I inspected the wall of the gorge, looking for a place to start my climb up. The sides of the gorge were extremely steep and lined with large boulders and jagged rocks. I couldn't see a place to go up, so I followed the river down even further until I found a place that was more passable. What I found looked like an overgrown trail but it would work.

A thick fog descended into the gorge as I made my way on the steep pathway. The fog was thick and visibility was low in front of me making the trees and landscape around me seem as if it were an eerie forest.

Much to my dismay, the trek up was proving to be much more difficult than the descent yesterday, and the conditions seemed to get worse as I moved on. There were many downed trees and thick vegetation that made it difficult to make my way.

I tried to stick to the path I had found, assuming it would lead me out of here. The path would appear and disappear on what seemed a whim, but it was a path and I was grateful for it.

The sun partially came out and the fog partially slipped away from in front of me. But the temperature remained cold.

After a few hours, I stopped for a rest on a ledge and looked out over the gorge. The sun was just beginning to peak out over the horizon, when the clouds rolled in. Within a few minutes the entire sky was covered with the same type of fogginess that had plagued me earlier.

I wondered if I might get caught in the rain on top of everything else.

I turned to start back on my climb and felt a little disoriented. I couldn't make out the path that I had been following.

I took a few steps, feeling around with my feet for solid ground, remembering the illusion of ground underneath the vegetation yesterday. I cautiously stepped forward, but to my horror my feet went straight through the brush and as if in slow motion, my body fell forward and straight over the cliff.

As my body fell through the air, I cried out, with only one thing on my mind.

Juliette.

I don't remember hitting the ground.

I was already gone.

CHAPTER 15

I WENT BACK INSIDE AFTER Liam left and tidied up a little. Everything was pretty much done from the check-out cleaning that I did yesterday, so I was done with the work within a short period of time.

I sat down on the edge of the bed and then got up and moved to the couch. After that I moved to the arm chair. I couldn't settle down and sit still.

I was feeling antsy and had to keep fighting the urge to worry about Liam.

I tried to keep the danger he was in, out of my head.

I knew he was strong and he was smart. If anyone could make it through the gorge, it was Liam.

In order to distract myself, I decided to go back to the blueberry bush in the meadow and see if I could find any remnant fruit.

I grabbed the red blanket and wrapped it around my shoulders like a shawl, before heading out the door.

I knew Liam wouldn't be back for hours yet, so I had time to kill.

I walked to the where the path opened up and stopped just on the edge of the woods.

I remembered Liam's words … "Stay out of the woods."

What seemed like a good idea, a few moments ago, now seemed like an ominous task.

Now that I was alone, the woods had regained their foreboding feel.

I looked anxiously back toward the cabin.

I considered the idea of going right back … but the thought of sitting there for hours, with nothing to do but worry, sounded more unappealing than the idea of facing the woods alone.

After all, I had gone alone to the meadow twice before. What was the difference now?

I stepped onto the path and entered the woods.

The sunlight filtered through the few remnant leaves on the trees, giving the lighting around me a speckled effect.

I wandered slowly down the path, taking in the beauty of the forest, as I was in no hurry to get back to the cabin.

I made my way quietly as squirrels scurried back and forth between trees. The wind rustled through the trees and dislodged more of the dead autumn leaves. I watched as they drifted in groups of two or three to the ground.

I looked up at the sky and could see patches of blue through the arms of the trees, waving in all their majesty.

A pair of blue jays screeched high up in the canopy of the tree limbs. I would occasionally catch a glimpse of their royal blue bodies as they flew in and out of view.

The foliage around me was thick and lush. I was surprised at how much green the forest retained, despite the cold autumn nights.

Large, knobby roots from ancient trees snaked their way across the forest floor, covered in billowy moss. Feathery ferns lined the path and brushed against my legs as I passed them.

The forest floor was damp from the morning dew. The musty smell of decaying leaves and wet pine needles filled my nose.

I walked almost in a dreamlike state, taking in the forest's magical feel.

Here, time seemed to slow and life took on a whole new meaning. It had its own world here, nothing outside of it seemed to matter.

When I finally reached the meadow, it was almost a shock to my eyes.

I had been so lost in the moment of swimming through the sea of trees behind me that I had almost forgotten where I was headed.

The broad sloping field was still a welcome sight.

It stood bright and was filled with a chorus of music, from songbirds flying and flitting about. They were joyously making their winter preparations.

I made my way along the edge of the meadow to the familiar bush and found it completely empty of fruit. I searched the ground and found a few withered up berries. I soon decided to abandon the idea. I wasn't hungry enough to eat rotten fruit. Not yet, anyway.

I sat on the edge of the meadow basking in the golden sunshine of autumn. I lay on my back and looked up at the clouds, as they floated gently across the ocean of blue sky.

I thought of Liam, knowing he was under this same sky, and wondered if he had made it to the gorge yet. Since, I didn't know what time it was, or how long he had been gone, I had no concept of where he could be right now.

I stared at the luminous clouds as they took the form of a horse, a car, a butterfly, and then I spotted one that looked like a person waving. I waved back.

My eyes grew heavy as I watched them magically changing form. Without even realizing that it was happening, I drifted off to sleep.

I awoke sometime later and stretched. I sat up quickly, disoriented. At first, I did not understand where I was. I squinted in the sunlight. Then, I heard the songbirds and the rustling of the tall meadow grasses in the breeze and realized I had fallen asleep in the meadow. I wondered how long I had been out?

I guessed it was early afternoon by the sun's position. It was directly overhead.

I jumped up and dusted myself off. I wanted to get back to the cabin as soon as possible.

I wanted to be there when Liam arrived.

I waited the rest of the afternoon, with high hopes, for him to return. As the minutes ticked away, I began to realize he might not make it back before dark. I kept staring at the opening of the drive. Willing him to come into view.

I sat on the front porch as the day drew to a close, feeling the last moments of sun's warmth before it disappeared completely. As the shadows moved across the yard, I woefully accepted the fact that Liam would not be returning today.

I went inside the cabin and added more wood to the fire. Just the way Liam had instructed me to do.

Then, I lit the stove and made myself a bowl of plain rice with the remnant grains left in the bag. I scoured the cabinets and drawers for anything to give it some flavor and came up empty handed. All I found was a rock hard artificial sweetener packet and an empty steak sauce bottle.

I took my rice and sat in front of the fire and ate it, pretending it was a huge bowl of broccoli and cheddar soup. When I was finished, I sat and read one of the newspapers that Liam had brought back from the lodge. I laughed at how times and prices had changed. The grocery flyer's prices were astonishing. A gallon of milk for $2.39 and a dozen eggs for 89 cents! I perused the wedding announcements and read an article about the rise of housing costs and one about the Galileo Spacecraft.

After I was finished with the paper, I watched the flames dancing in the fireplace, until I grew sleepy again. I lay down on the couch and covered myself with the red blanket. I quickly fell asleep. Pushing the thoughts of the possibility of Liam being outside in the gorge after dark ... and the fact that I was alone in the middle of the wilderness ... as far out of my mind as possible.

I tossed and turned the whole night in a dreamless sleep.

CHAPTER 16

DAY 2 ALONE

THE DAY DAWNED GREY. I looked out the window and the yard was covered in a low lying mist, giving it a dreamlike appearance.

I dressed as quickly as I could in my blue jeans and yellow sweater and ran out onto the porch to wait for Liam and the rescuers.

The air was even colder than yesterday and I had a difficult time keeping warm. I refused to go back inside, I wanted to see Liam as soon as he arrived.

Within an hour the mist had turned to a dense fog and I could no longer see, not even to the wood line.

I went back inside the cabin grimly knowing that Liam and the rescuers would have to wait until the fog lifted to come for me.

While I waited, I decided to whip up some of those pancakes that Liam had made a few days ago. They weren't the tastiest things in the world, but I was hungry and I needed something to occupy myself with anyway.

I sang pieces of songs that I could remember by heart while I pulled out the flour, sugar, and baking soda. I twirled around and danced to songs in my head as I poured them into a mixing bowl. Then, I poured some of my bottled water in, careful to not use too much. I mixed it up with a fork and after I had made a decent looking batter, I tried to light the stove.

I turned the switch and nothing happened.

I tried two more times before I finally realized what was wrong.

I was out of propane.

There would be no pancakes for breakfast.

I tried to eat the raw batter but gagged on it.

It was disgusting. I took it to the woods and dumped it out.

I went back inside the cabin and looked through the food that I had left.

Two cans of chicken noodle soup, a package of noodles, two snack bags of gummy bears, and a small unopened bag of sunflower seeds, that I had brought from home.

There wasn't much left at all. Without being able to cook anything now either, things were even less opportune.

I hoped even more that Liam would be here tonight. My stomach growled in protest at the thought of my inventory of meal choices.

My mind wandered to what I would get to eat, when we were rescued. I thought of spaghetti, hamburgers, and tacos. My mouth watered and my stomach growled even louder.

I went to the window and looked out. The fog had completely lifted though the sky was still overcast and grey.

I wondered if it might rain.

Either way, I was happy. I knew the rescuers could come now. Even if it did rain, they could still come.

My mind immediately went to Liam.

They would come … if Liam had made it to the general store.

I found myself beginning to worry again. I wondered if he had made it safely through the gorge. I had to keep reassuring myself that all was well. I had to believe that. There was no reason not to.

After all, I had complete confidence in his abilities.

So, once again, I pushed the fears out of my mind, despite the nagging feeling in my gut that something was wrong.

I continued to believe he would return at any moment and that is what got me through the first five days alone.

The fear that he wasn't coming back for me began to slowly eat at me, from the inside out, as I attempted to fight it off.

I would not let it enter the realm of possibility.

I refused to give up hope.

So, day in and day out, I waited.

… and waited.

CHAPTER 17

DAY 6 ALONE

I AWOKE JUST BEFORE dawn. The room was dark but I could see out the window, a streak of pink from the start of sunrise. I looked over in the direction of the fireplace and there was nothing but darkness. The fire was out. I shivered as I pulled back the covers in the darkness and a wave of ice cold hit me.

I couldn't believe I had slept through the night.

The last few nights had been awful. I lay completely awake each night wishing sleep would come, but it evaded me, leaving me listening to every creak, crack and bang in the night. Every sound was amplified.

Each morning, my spirits would be high again, in expectation of Liam's return, but by the afternoon, my mood would dim as the sun would set and darkness ascended around the cabin.

Each day the same as the one before.

I got up as the sun rose to a bright and beautiful morning. The cold had seemed to recede and the air had turned nicer again during the day making the waiting more bearable. The warm sunshine of the morning pushed away all the cold from the cabin, as I slowly dressed for the day, in clothes that I was sure by now, smelled terrible. Although I couldn't smell anything myself, I could only guess that I was accustomed to the odor they were bound to have.

Up until today, I had been satisfied with the waiting, despite the long nights, but now I sat at the table sipping on my last bottle of water and the quiet, unspoken truth surrounded me.

I stared at nothing, as a numbing grief encompassed me.

I felt so lost and utterly alone.

Where was Liam?

Was he hurt?

Was he dead?

Had he left me here, so he could be with Susan?

The questions ran rampant in my head making me dizzy.

I had pushed the thought of him possibly not returning for me, as far away as possible for as long as possible … but the thought nagged at me this morning.

No matter how hard I tried to not think about it, it wouldn't leave me alone.

Once I allowed it to enter my thoughts, it took off like a wildfire, out of control. Ice cold panic set in and I shook involuntarily, from head to toe.

I stood up from the table and took off running as fast as I could, out the front door of the cabin, and into the woods.

I didn't stop until I was standing in the middle of my meadow.

The pale-yellow grasses blowing in the wind around me.

The thought of Liam not returning had seeped into every square inch of my being and I screamed at the top of my lungs.

The sound of it made a nearby flock of birds take sudden flight, making a roaring whooshing sound over my head.

I screamed out, repeating the words:

"He's not coming back!"

"He's not coming back!"

"He's not coming back!"

I screamed until I couldn't scream anymore and the words were hoarse whispers.

"Oh God, he's not coming back … "

I fell down on my knees in the dirt and sobbed.

I cried for Liam.

I cried for Janie.

I cried for myself and my lost life.

I was a dead man walking. I was going to die here, alone in the wilderness.

I lay down on the ground and sobbed until the tears were gone and I was left with nothing but dry sobs.

I don't know how much time had passed with me lying there in my grief induced coma. When I finally opened my eyes, the sun was high in the sky.

I stood up and dusted myself off and slowly headed back toward the path. My head ached from all the crying.

I could feel my eyes were swollen and my throat was sore from screaming.

I walked slowly, almost in a daze.

Just as I was about to enter the woods, something bright yellow in the brush caught my eye. I stopped and looked again.

It was definitely a streak of bright yellow.

It seemed so out of place here, so I walked over to have a closer look.

Deep under a dry, withered bush was a little yellow bird. As I got closer, I could see better. It was a yellow canary with light black striping on its wings.

It was injured and I could see it was terrified of me, as I approached it.

I lowered myself to the ground and spoke softly. It looked up at me with fearful eyes, blinking.

I scooped it up gingerly in my hands. Its body was light and definitely underweight.

I wondered how long it had been under there.

I thought how ironic it was that we had both been left here to die.

I held the small bird against my chest and carried it back to the cabin with me.

I decided I would do whatever I could to help it.

Glad to have something to give me a little bit of purpose again.

I was familiar with canaries.

My grandmother lived in England and I spent several summers with her when I was young. She raised yellow canaries. They flew all over her house. She loved those beautiful yellow birds.

She had a special conservatory filled with plants, built just for them to live in. It was a magical place. I felt like it was my very own secret garden. The plants grew tall and the whole place radiated with the songs of the canaries.

I would spend hours in the conservatory.

One of my favorite things about being in there, was when the canaries would come and land around me. Slowly at first, but then soon, I could hold out birdseed and they would eat it directly from my hand.

My grandmother would watch from a distance, smiling. She enjoyed the fact, that I loved them too.

She taught me all about the history of these beautiful little birds.

The small songbirds originally came from the Macaronesian Islands and were originally green finches. They were first domesticated in the 1400's for their graceful singing. They were bred for hundreds of years to get that sunshine yellow color.

My grandmother was not religious but she was a very spiritual woman who believed in symbolism and signs. I believe that this was one of the reasons why she was so enamored with them.

Canaries had a long history in spiritual symbolism. They were joyful birds that were known to spread happiness and a sense of overall well-being. For some, spotting a flying canary could even be a sign of freedom for them.

The legend said a canary would appear to you when you were in need of healing from old wounds that were still lingering. It would come to teach you that you were stronger and wiser than you realized.

The canary was said to usher in light, inspiration, and joyful energy. They would signal to you the arrival of a new cycle or journey, as you broke away from the old and started to tell a new story. This light would bring a new view filled with grace and love. It would fill your spirit with bliss, even if it was just for a moment. That moment would stay engraved in your heart forever.

My grandmother believed in the light of the divine and in that light, you could be healed and renewed. All you had to do was open your arms and allow the light inside.

I remembered running around the yard with my arms wide open willing the light to shine on me, in the hopes I might take flight like the canaries. I would close my eyes and run while the wind whipped through my hair.

It wasn't beyond me, that at this very point in my life, I had come upon this injured canary. I half laughed because I knew what my grandmother would have said about it.

My best memories of my childhood were of the time I spent with my grandmother. To me she was the most magical person that ever lived.

She had long gray hair that went to her waist. She always kept it twisted up in a perfect bun, that showed off the very same eyes that Jacko and I had. It was only at night, right before bed, that I would get to see her with her hair completely down. She would run a brush through it and the silver streaks would sparkle in the light.

She was my mother's mother. They never had a very close relationship but I loved her with my whole heart.

I was left there with her when my parents would go on their summertime continuing education retreats. They would be gone for eight weeks or more but I didn't mind.

She lived in a small cottage on a cobblestone street. Her house was situated in the beautiful English countryside where the color green was given new meaning. There was nothing I had seen before or since that time, that could compare to the lush green there.

We would spend the days working in her garden and tending to the flower beds. On the days it rained, we would put together puzzles and bake cookies and bread to share with the neighbors. When the sun would come back out, we would walk hand in hand down the cobblestone road to deliver the goodies. I still could remember how soft her hands were.

She was the gentlest person I had ever known. She was a natural born encourager.

When we would talk about my future, she would always say how much she believed in me.

She told me I was special and had a purpose in this world. That we all do.

As a child, I was filled with wonder and imagination of what that purpose would be.

Now, I doubted if I had any purpose at all.

My faith in life was dwindling to a low flicker.

I found a small cardboard box in one of the cabinets in the cabin and placed the canary in it. I also put a towel folded up on the bottom for her to have something soft to lie on.

I poured some of my water into a jar lid and put it in the box with her.

I didn't know what was wrong, but I wasn't going to let her die alone, out there in the cold.

I hated to put her in the box because I knew canaries were very sensitive to their environment. They would not even sing in a dark cage, but she needed security and quiet.

This was the best I could do for her.

I built my fire for the night while still rolling over the memories of my grandmother.

She died when I was fourteen and I never quite got over it. It was one of the darkest times of my life.

I wished so many times for her, after Jacko died.

She would've known exactly what to say to pull me out of the darkness.

I went into the kitchen and searched the empty cabinets for something to make for dinner. There wasn't much of anything left, so I went to bed hungry. Which was the norm these days.

I peeked in the box to check on the canary before I went to bed and she was sleeping with her head tucked neatly under her wing.

She looked so peaceful.

I was so glad I had decided to bring her back with me.

I said another silent prayer for her recovery.

I crawled in the bed and stared at the firelight dancing on the ceiling. I kept thinking of Liam.

I called out to him in the darkness.

"Where are you, Liam?"

"Where are you … ?" I whimpered.

The wind rattled the tin roof above me, making the hair on the back of my neck stand up.

I could hear rustling noises outside of the cabin and I wondered, in terror, what was out there. Bears, wolves, mountain lions …

I cried myself to sleep with Liam's name on my lips.

CHAPTER 18

I AWOKE WITH THE WILL to survive pulsing through me.

Hoping against hope, that Liam would still somehow return. My heart was heavy with grief, but I pushed it out of the way and let hope reside there instead.

I wasn't ready to give up yet.

My supplies had dwindled quickly, including wood for the fire.

I had half of a bottle of water left and even though I had barely eaten anything at all, the food that I had left was pretty much gone too. All I had left was a half of a bag of sunflower seeds.

I knew I would have to make a trip to the lodge for supplies. I was terrified of going alone but if I didn't, I would starve to death. I was already extremely weak from barely eating.

I checked on the little bird, who I symbolically decided to name Hope. I was thankful to see her bright eyes when I peered inside the box. She blinked at me as I dropped a few of my sunflower seeds down in the box with her. I hoped the will to eat would kick in. If she ate, I knew she would pull through this injury. Her water was a little dirty, so I knew it was quite possible she had drunk some of it.

I walked outside on the porch and looked over at the woodpile. I needed to cut some firewood, so I went over and picked up the axe. It was much heavier than I expected it to be. I set a log up on its side on top of another log, just like I had seen Liam do.

I lifted the axe over my head and swung it at the log. The axe's weight lurched me violently forward and then stabbed into the ground, missing the log entirely.

My eyes were wide open with shock. I was thankful it hadn't kicked back and gotten me in the leg instead.

I lifted the axe again and steadied myself. This time, when I swung, the axe came down in the center of the log. Dead in the center, giving me a burst of pride. I whooped with joy.

The feeling was short lasting. I couldn't get the axe back out. It was stuck in the log. I dragged it around the yard, trying to dislodge the axe and couldn't do it. After twenty minutes of trying, I gave up. As far as I was concerned, it was permanently wedged in the log. I didn't have the strength to pull it out.

Liam had made it look so easy …

I sat down on one of the logs and cried. I felt completely helpless.

I didn't have to worry about food anymore because I would freeze to death! The nights were getting colder and without a fire, I would surely get hypothermia.

Suddenly, I remembered the wood pile we had seen at the lodge. The wood was old and dry, but it would burn and keep me warm!

I jumped up and went inside the cabin to get my tote bag and headed for the lodge.

The walk took me a while longer than it had Liam and me during our previous treks.

My stamina was low due to lack of food and adequate water but I still made it there by early afternoon.

The lodge was a welcome sight. I went inside and closed the door behind me. Once inside, I looked around nervously. It felt a little creepier without Liam here with me.

The thought of Liam immediately made tears start to sting my eyes.

I pushed them back. I couldn't afford to lose control right now. I had a limited amount of time before the sun would set.

I looked around the lodge and found a cabinet filled with miscellaneous items. There was no rhyme or reason to what was in there. I grabbed a box of candles, matches with green foil backing that read 'La Siesta est. 1965', and a crossword puzzle book.

I put them all in my tote bag.

I searched through another cabinet and found a first aid kit, vintage shaving kit, and a bar of Irish Spring soap.

I pulled out the soap, brought it to my nose and took a whiff. The scent was still strong.

Memories of my father swirled through my mind. This was the soap he always used when I was a little girl. He would smell just like this, in the mornings, before he left to go to the office.

I took the soap and put it my bag. I knew I desperately needed it. I half laughed at the understatement.

Next, I went into the kitchen and dug through the cabinets. I grabbed a bag of dry beans, more rice, a canister of oats, and a bottle of expired mustard.

To my delight, in the back of one of the cabinets, I found an old metal tea kettle and a cannister of tea.

Then, I opened another cabinet and pulled down the expired canned food that Liam had told me to put back, when we were here last.

There was hash, tomato and beef pasta, tuna, and several cans of potted meat.

My mouth instantly watered. I grabbed the can of beef pasta and fished through the drawers frantically, until I found a can opener. I opened it and sniffed. It smelled fine ... and I was starving. I chose to ignore Liam's words of warning. I sunk a spoon into the can and took a big bite. An intense sour and salty flavor washed over my tongue and I almost gagged. I wasn't used to canned pasta. I swallowed without chewing. I just needed to get it down. After I finished the entire can, I felt a little nauseated but better overall, now that I had a little nutrition in my system.

I packed several of the cans in my bag with the other items. The bag was pretty heavy now, so I decided to pull out the oats, beans and rice. I took the cans instead, since I had no way to cook the dried goods, anyway.

I went to a small room that was just adjacent to the great room and opened the door. Liam had said he thought it was a smoking room. The walls were made of wood paneling that was painted a mossy green color. There were large glass ashtrays and a felt topped poker table. A giant catfish was mounted on the wall over a bricked wood burning fireplace. Along the opposite wall was a large built in bookshelf filled with books. I gasped with delight.

I couldn't believe that I hadn't noticed it, when we were here before!

I ran my hand along the hundreds of books that lined the shelves. Most were hardback and leather bound.

I felt like I had just won the lottery.

There was *Lord of the Flies, To Kill a Mockingbird, A Tale of Two Cities, Moby Dick, The Scarlett Letter*, and so many more!

I read through the titles, wishing I could take them all. I grabbed two of them, *The Scarlett Letter and Moby Dick*.

Just as I was about to turn away, a worn green hardback book with frayed edges, caught my eye.

I couldn't believe my eyes!

It was an old copy of *Jane Eyre*; the title was written in gold lettering down the spine.

I grabbed the book and held it to my chest.

My childhood favorite! It had been years since I had read it.

Seeing it, made me feel like I had run into an old friend.

This time I choked back tears of joy.

I packed my three books in my bag and looked around for something to help me filter water. I knew they had to have something here, since there wasn't running water in the lodge. I couldn't imagine they hauled water in every time they came.

I checked every single room, coming up empty handed with each try.

As I checked the last closet I noticed a small door in the back of it, hidden behind some coats.

I unhooked the latch and opened the door. The dank musty smell of a cellar went up my nose. I peered down into the darkness, with my heart beating wildly in my chest.

I knew I needed to go down there.

I had never liked dark places. I was terrified of the dark, growing up and somehow being alone like this had reignited my childhood fear.

My imagination ran away with me, thinking of what could be down there.

Snakes, spiders, ghosts … …

Terror ran through me.

I backed out of the closet and stared at it for several minutes, until the resolve to find a way to filter water got stronger than my fear.

I had checked everywhere else.

The cellar was my last hope.

I got one of the candles out of my bag and lit it.

I took a deep breath before I started down the stairs of the cellar.

The dank smell overpowered me as I made my way down the steps. I trembled with fear as I held the candle up, trying to see what was around me.

Suddenly, I heard a loud scurrying sound and I screamed so loud it echoed in the cellar.

I tried to look in the direction of the noise but couldn't see much of anything.

Then, without warning, a large rat ran past my feet and up the side of the damp wall.

I let out a deafening scream.

I had to fight every urge to run back up the steps.

I backed away from the place where the rat had disappeared. As I stepped backwards, I tripped over something and fell to the ground. My candle flickered like it might go out, as I tried to see what I had fallen on. My imagination went wild, believing I had fallen over a dead body. When my eyes finally adjusted, I could see what it was.

I was almost in shock. It was a five-gallon jug of water. There were at least 10 of them down here! I couldn't believe my good fortune.

I grabbed one of them by the neck and hauled it back up the steps into the lodge with me.

The bottle was glass and had a faded label on it that read: *Blue Mountain Water, Naturally Sourced.*

As much as I wanted to open it right there and drink a big glass, I knew I needed to get it back to the cabin with me, unopened. In the case that I couldn't get it closed tightly again, it could leak water on the way back and I needed every single drop.

Suddenly, it dawned on me, how *would* I transport this jug of water back ... and not to mention all the firewood that I needed?

How would I get it all back to the cabin? I didn't even know how I was going to carry the tote bag with cans and books, as it was.

I hadn't even thought of that fact until this moment.

I racked my brain. There had to be a way to transport this weight without me carrying it all. Suddenly, the idea of using a blanket as a wagon of sorts, came to me. I could drag it behind me, with the wood and water, loaded on it.

I grabbed a large green blanket from one of the closets and went outside with my haul, to evaluate the wood.

The wood pile was pretty large. There was enough chopped wood there to get me through a good while.

I spread the blanket on the ground and put the water in the center.

Then, I started stacking wood pieces around it.

I felt pretty good about things until I looked down at my hand. As I was pulling a piece of wood from the stack, I saw a huge black widow spider crawling up my hand.

I shrieked so loud, I was certain it could be heard for miles.

I imagined my scream echoing through the valley.

I violently shook the spider off of my hand and it scurried back into the wood pile, unscathed.

After that, I was too terrified to put my hand back in the wood pile.

I looked up at the sky and the sun was shifting. I knew I had spent too much time here anyway.

From what I could tell, I had enough wood to last a couple of days, so I decided to head back with my treasures. I tied the corners of the blanket together and threw my tote bag on my shoulder. The weight of the tote bag alone, made my shoulder ache immensely. I set the bag down and took out the cans and added them to the blanket.

When I lifted the tote bag back onto my shoulder, it was much more comfortable.

I grabbed the tied part of the blanket and dragged it along behind me. The first few minutes, I was super proud of myself and marched along with a smile, but within a short while, I grew weary under the load.

I went downhill and fast. My body had almost no strength left.

I wanted to stop but I kept dragging it along, knowing I had no other choice.

My legs quivered and my arms ached. My shoulder felt like it was breaking under the weight of the tote bag, despite removing the cans.

I stopped and shoved it into the blanket pouch too, thinking it would be easier to pull than carry.

I felt a little rejuvenated from the weight being off of my shoulder but immediately fatigue began to overtake me again.

I couldn't go on.

I had only made it about half way and I was exhausted.

I stopped there on the path and fell to the ground crying. Self-pity and debilitating fatigue had overtaken me.

I sat on my knees and sobbed.

I remembered the old saying, mind over matter, but I didn't believe it.

I just couldn't go on. I was giving up. It was over.

I was still crying, when I heard a sound just to my left, through the trees. Branches crackled and I could hear the distinct sound of something moving through the woods.

Something big.

The image of the bear that Liam and I saw ran through my mind's eye.

I just knew it was back … and it was after me.

I shot to standing in a blink and with the fear pumping adrenalin through my body, I dragged the blanket all the way back to the cabin without stopping once.

If I had only looked behind me, I would have seen a raccoon meander out onto the path just as I disappeared out of sight.

I arrived at the cabin, just before dusk.

I brought in enough wood for the night along with my treasured books and water jug.

After I got everything I needed inside, I checked on Hope. She was still lying in the same place. She hadn't moved since this morning. Her water and sunflower seeds were untouched.

"Come on little girl … " I whispered to her.

The sun was fully set, so I lit a candle.

I went to the table and was emptying my tote bag, when a wave of nausea washed over me.

That wave was quickly followed by another wave and with it, stomach cramps, like I had never felt before.

My gut turned inside out and I was dizzy from the pain.

I barely made it out the front door before I vomited. I fell down on my knees on the ground in the darkness and vomited until nothing else would come out. I dry heaved, while the convulsions pulsed through my abdomen. I cried out from the excruciating pain.

Not long after I stopped vomiting, the diarrhea began. I passed every bit of the can of beef pasta and then some.

I felt so sick and weak, I thought surely, I would die.

I spent the next few hours, lying on the grass, moaning, while the convulsions worked their way through me.

I wasn't aware of anything until much later in the night. The ground under me was hard and cold. I stirred not understanding where I was, until I heard the sound of a hoot owl coming from the woods. I jolted up and ran inside the house.

I crawled into my bed and slept the rest of the night without waking.

CHAPTER 19

I WOKE UP WITH MY HEAD pounding and a strong metallic taste in my mouth. I was still a little nauseated, though most of the food poisoning had worked its way through my system.

Liam had been right to warn me about the canned food.

Now, I wished I had listened to his words.

I stood up and the room spun. I knew I was badly dehydrated, so I grabbed my water bottle and guzzled down the last of it, inspiring a new wave of convulsions. I immediately realized, that I should've taken the water in more slowly.

I doubled over with the pain but successfully fought the urge to vomit again.

After my stomach settled, I took all the cans of rotten food and bagged them up.

Now, I was back at square one.

No food.

I had just enough strength to make it back to the meadow to pick up the leftover berries off of the ground. I nibbled on the withered berries. They were tart and sweet. Their flavor was very close to that of raisins. I gathered the rest of them up and put them in my bag for later.

I decided to take the long way back around the meadow, just to explore a little. I thought maybe I might find another blueberry bush.

As I followed along the edge of the meadow, I listened to the birds singing in the trees. I ran my hand along the tops of the tall grass as I walked. The wind blew through them making a swooshing sound.

A fox darted out of the woods, startling me. It stopped directly in front of me. His long red fur blew majestically in the wind. His eyes were a striking golden yellow color. He looked around, not seeming to notice me at all. Then, our eyes met for just a moment before he bounded off and disappeared into the grasses of the meadow.

As I stood staring at the spot where he disappeared, I realized I could hear something in the distance.

It was the distinct tinkling sound of water trickling and bubbling in a creek.

I followed the sound along a leaf carpeted path, until I reached a narrow, slow flowing creek with deep pools of clear water.

There were logs and downed branches that created small natural waterfalls that babbled and splashed over them, with seeming delight.

The water flowed along, as it gurgled and spat over scattered stones.

I had never seen anything so beautiful.

I looked over at the place where the water had formed a large clear pool. Through the water I could see smooth earth toned river rocks.

It beckoned to me … and I was thrilled. I could bathe in there! Oh, how long it had been since I had showered! A luxury I was missing, almost as much as food.

I quickly ran back to the cabin and grabbed my bar of Irish Spring, the cleanest clothes I had, and a towel and rushed back to the creek.

When I got back the water was even more of a beautiful sight.

The stream twisted and turned gently through the forest with large rocks edging the sides with fluffy green moss on top.

It seemed to have no end or beginning.

It just existed in the beauty of its surroundings.

I stripped off my clothes and stepped down into the crystal pools of water. The coldness of it shocked me but the lure of getting clean, kept me moving forward. I slipped down into the water and let out a little shriek. Soon my body became accustomed to the cold temperature and I spun around and twirled in the water. I grabbed the soap and washed my hair, my face, and my body.

I sighed with delight. I never knew a bath could feel so good!

After I was clean, I got out, toweled off, and dressed with the clothes I brought with me.

I sat on one of the rocks and shivered from the cold, but I relished the feeling of being clean. I ran a brush through my hair, as I kept sniffing my hands. The clean smell of soap, still on them.

Enjoying the moment so intently, I temporarily forgot the state in which I was living.

I forgot for just a moment, that I was alone ... and starving in the wilderness.

As I made my way back to the cabin, I felt a little woozy. So, I decided it was best to wait until tomorrow to go back to the lodge to get the dried food that I had left behind.

I was too weak and needed to regain a little strength before going back.

I was hungry but it felt a lot better than being sick.

I settled in one of the front porch rockers and opened up the copy of *Jane Eyre* that I had found.

I began reading and suddenly all my troubles drifted away. I was lost for hours within the pages of the old familiar story.

Before I knew it, the sun was getting low in the sky. I closed the book, went inside, and made the evening fire.

I checked on Hope. Nothing had changed and my fear for her grew. She sat looking at me with blinking eyes. I pleaded with her silently, to get well.

I refilled my water bottle and climbed into my lonely bed.

I looked over at the empty side where Liam had once slept and began to cry.

Another day had come and gone and he hadn't returned.

My hope was growing dimmer.

CHAPTER 20

I WOKE UP FEELING MORE alone than I ever had been.

I ached for Liam.

I ached for Janie.

Ever since that first moment, when I found out that I was pregnant and discovered there was life growing inside of me, I was enthralled with the idea of having a permanent companion.

Each little flutter of life thrilled me beyond measure.

Flash forward a year from that moment and I found myself in those parenting moments where I would've given anything for five minutes alone.

Now here I am.

Alone.

No one pulling at my shirt, no one calling my name.

When I was younger, I thought I would never want to be a mom but once I had the twins, all that changed.

I loved being a mother more than anything I had ever done before in my life. It gave me back a piece of my life that I had forgotten existed. Seeing the world through their eyes brought magic back into my world. Dragons, fairies, and dinosaurs walked among us. The joy of daily songs and patty cake. The rediscovered delight of ice cream cones, water sprinklers, and Christmas. I lived in a world where eating a chocolate chip cookie was something to be celebrated, in and of itself.

Their smiles, their laughter … it all made life worth living.

I closed my eyes and could see Janie, smiling. I could see the memory as clear as it if it was happening right in front of me.

She was wearing a red polka dot dress with white smocking across the chest. She had a giant red bow in her hair. The breeze was blowing her curls in her face and she was laughing.

Her delight was in chasing the squirrels around that were gathering acorns for the winter.

It was the Saturday before we left for this trip and I had taken her to the park to play in the warm autumn sun. I sat on a blanket, in the grass, under a giant oak tree, whose leaves had turned a vibrant yellow. I felt as if I were sitting under a tree of sunshine.

I sat there and watched her embrace all that life had to offer.

It was a good day.

A really good day.

I wished that somehow, I could transport myself right back to that moment.

Just to be back with Janie, even if it was only in my dreams. If I could just fall back asleep, I could at least dream about being with her again.

I couldn't imagine what she must be thinking and feeling right now.

Mommy and Daddy never came home.

Tears spilled down onto the pillow, as the morning sun shone brightly into the cabin through the tattered curtains.

I didn't want to get up. What reason did I have?

As if on cue, my stomach growled and let me know in no uncertain terms that I needed food and I needed it soon.

I thought about the market we had stopped at on our way here. I ashamedly remembered how I had been so prejudiced against the selections they offered. What I wouldn't give right now, to have anything at all in that shop. At this point, I would even be willing to eat the mystery eggs in the jar that I had seen at the register.

The thought of that, almost made me laugh.

Almost.

I got up and slipped on my jeans. I had grown thin and they were baggy now. I had always wanted to try to lose the baby weight, but this wasn't the diet idea that I had in mind. That was for sure.

I checked on Hope and she fluttered her wings at me when I peeked in the box.

A very good sign.

Then, I noticed that a few sunflower shells were cracked open, meaning she had eaten.

Another good sign.

I headed out in the morning air and started off to the lodge.

I was weak but pushed myself forward and got there in a decent amount of time. When I got inside, I went down into the cellar and brought several of the water jugs up into the lodge.

I did not want to have to go in the cellar every time I needed water. I hated going down there.

Afterwards, I went into the kitchen and carefully dug through the cabinets to ensure I didn't miss anything in there that I could potentially eat. I came up empty handed. So, I took the dry goods that I originally left behind and put them in my bag. I would have to find a way to make them edible.

I found myself actually beginning to believe the entire lodge and all of its contents in general, were mine.

I believed it was placed here just for me, and me alone. An oasis of sorts. I had stopped thinking of it as borrowing supplies. In my delirium, I felt they were mine for the taking.

In fact, if it hadn't been so run down, I would have just moved right in but the cabin was way more habitable at this point.

I went into the smoking room to look at the books again. My own personal library.

I perused the bookshelves and stumbled on a small red leather-bound book. I pulled it out and engraved in gold, on the leather front cover, was the word *Journal.*

I opened it up and found that it was filled with beautiful handwriting, scribbled on now yellowed pages.

I saw the words ... *So, no one forgets* ... written on the dedication page, all alone.

Nothing else was written on that one page.

I was immediately intrigued. I closed the journal and put it in my bag. I could read more later.

I looked around for some rope too. I wanted a way to make a drying line for my clothes. I knew I could use the bar soap and hand wash them. Luckily, I found a rolled ball of twine on a shelf in the main room, which would work perfectly.

Just before I headed out the door, I saw the fishing rods. I remembered the fish that Liam had caught and cooked for us. My mouth watered at the thought.

I had never fished myself. I had only been a spectator but it couldn't be that hard ... or could it?

I grabbed one of the rods, not thinking about the fact that we were out of propane.

Hunger was driving.

I took the rod down to the river. It took me, what I guessed was an hour, to figure out how to cast it into the water. I just kept flinging it and couldn't understand why the line wouldn't come out until I finally discovered the release button. After a few tries, I got it into the water. I sat down on a rock and waited. And waited. And waited.

Nothing happened.

I reeled it back in and recast it out again.

The same thing happened.

I just couldn't understand why it wasn't working and then suddenly I realized why.

No bait.

I went back up to the lodge and found a lure. I tied it onto the end of the line and tried again.

This time within a few minutes I felt a tug and reeled my line in but there was no fish.

I cast it in again and this time when I felt something, the tug was stronger and then it turned into a pull. I could feel there was definitely something on the line!

I reeled and reeled against the weight and suddenly a trout appeared. I shouted for joy as I reeled him all the way onto the bank.

He flopped violently on the ground and when I reached down to pick him up, his body was so slimy that he slipped right out of my hands. It took several attempts before I was able to get a good hold on him. I pulled the hook out of his mouth. His eyes were wide and his gills gaped open as he struggled to breathe.

My heart sank.

He wanted to live just as much as I did.

I looked back at the lodge where I knew the dry foods were. Then, looked back him in defeat. I teared up. I knew I couldn't kill him. Not now. Not when I had other options for food.

I grimly realized when the food ran out, it would be a different story, but for now I couldn't do it.

I bent over the water's edge and slipped him back into the river.

As I headed back up to the lodge, something black shot across the path almost across my feet. It was a long black snake. Its skin shimmered in the sunlight as it crossed in front of me. I screamed and, in my fear, I stumbled forward over a root. I fell to the ground and face planted in the dirt. As soon as I hit the ground, a startled water bird flew out from some nearby brush squawking loudly.

With the sound of beating wings so loud just above me, I covered my head. After the bird was gone, I stood up. As

I dusted off, I saw the place where she had flown out from. There was a nest with several eggs.

I nearly leapt for joy!

Eggs!!

There were three speckled eggs, glistening in the sunlight. I gingerly lifted them up and took them with me back to the lodge.

I sent a silent apology to the mother bird who would soon come back to an empty nest.

Guilt wouldn't get the best of me this time.

I got back to the cabin sometime in the mid-afternoon.

I couldn't move fast enough. I was anticipating the buttery flavor of the eggs. I had remembered on the walk back that we still had charcoal for the grill and I couldn't wait to cook these up.

I brought a cast iron frying pan outside and set it on the porch. Then, I dragged the grill around to the front and opened the lid to get the charcoal bag that Liam had been storing inside of the grill.

As I lifted the bag, I realized in horror that the bag was empty, aside from two or three leftover briskets.

I sat down on the ground in defeat.

Just as I was about to have a meltdown, the image of a primitive hearth stove, that I had read about in a book, came into my mind.

It was built over a fire with bricks stacked up on each side and a grate over the top.

It was something that I could easily re-create and make my own indoor grill!

Within renewed determination, I searched the property for bricks or flat rocks. After a while, I had found enough to satisfy me. I went inside to the fireplace and built up two rock walls. Then, I brought in the grate from the outside grill and put it on top.

It had a distinct slant to it, but it would work!

I told the good news to Hope, who blinked back at me with bright eyes.

I cooked one egg and put the other two on the counter. The first bite was heavenly. I couldn't remember anything ever tasting so good. I savored every bite of the rich buttery flavor. When it was gone, I started a pot of barley. I was careful to make just enough for one meal because I didn't have any way to store leftovers.

That night I went to bed with an empty heart and full stomach.

CHAPTER 21

DAY 10 ALONE

MY HOPE WAS FADING. The idea that Liam was never coming back had taken root. There was no way it would have taken him ten days to get help.

I knew there was only one reason, and one reason alone, that he wouldn't have returned by now ...

The crushing truth could no longer be ignored. Terrifying images of Liam falling to his death in the gorge overwhelmed me.

I tried to push the images out of my mind, but I couldn't keep them away.

I knew in my heart that Liam was dead.

He would have never left me alone like this.

Only death would have stopped him.

My son was dead ... and now my husband was dead too.

I had lost two of the people that I loved most in the world.

... and I was left here alone.

Abandoned in the wilderness.

Grief overtook me and I lay in the bed and cried for hours, only getting up once to check on Hope and make sure she had food and water.

Terrifying images swirled through my mind. My head spun with sights and sounds that my mind conjured up about Liam's fate. As much as I tried, I couldn't make them stop. Anguish pulsed through me. When my mind finally settled, I just stared at the wall.

Sometime in the late afternoon, I got up and walked outside.

I stood in the middle of the yard. My emotions whirled out of control.

I was terrified ... and grief stricken.

I looked around wildly, at the forest surrounding me.

"I need you Liam!" I called out into the air.

"Where are you!?"

"Oh God ... where are you?" I sobbed.

"PLEASE Liam! Please! I need you to come back to me!" My voice reached its highest pitch.

"How you could leave me alone like this!?"

"LIAM!!" I screamed out as loud as I could.

His name and my sobs echoed through the forest.

I sunk to my knees with my face in my hands, knowing I would never see my husband again.

CHAPTER 22

DAY 11 ALONE

I GOT UP AROUND DAWN and put on a pot to cook the oats for my breakfast. A luxury I had not intended on affording myself. I planned to keep my meals to just one a day to make sure I had enough food until someone found me.

This morning, I just didn't care. A numbing depression had overtaken me.

I didn't care about rationing. I didn't care about survival.

I sat at the table while it cooked, staring out at nothing, paralyzed with grief.

Hope looked up at me from her box. She had gotten a little more active, so I knew she was starting to heal.

After breakfast, I took her out to get some fresh air. She lifted her head and poked her beak in the air, almost as if she was basking in the sunlight.

She had gotten used to me holding her now, as I had picked her up a few times to clean her box. She was eating the seeds every day and drinking her water. I was so happy to see her recovering. It was my only ray of light.

I wished she would sing like my grandmother's canaries did, but I knew as long as she was trapped in that cardboard box, she wouldn't.

After a while I took her back inside and gathered up my dirty clothes. I took them out on the porch and washed them in a bucket. The water was cold and my hands ached but I didn't care.

I wrung them out and hung them up to dry on a line that had I strung across the porch with the twine I had found at the lodge.

I now had a new respect for the women of the past who had washed all their clothes this way.

After the laundry was hung up and drying, I did my daily chores of bringing in wood and tidying up the cabin.

I no longer saw the cabin as lovely and charming. I felt as if it was a prison of sorts and I was its prisoner. Left here to die. Even though I knew someone would come and find me here eventually, I didn't know how long it would be and

I realized, the reality of me surviving the winter out here, was slim to none.

My supplies were running low. Even the lodge was almost out of everything.

I was out of choices and running out of time.

After my lunch of rice with mustard, I picked up my book to go outside and read.

Before I even reached the door, a gust of wind blew through the open window next to me and rattled the dry rotted screen.

The tattered thin curtain swirled around wildly, as if it were dancing.

I looked outside and the sky had turned a deep grey.

I went out and felt my clothes. They were still wet.

I looked up as a black bank of clouds moved in overhead.

The first roll of thunder was soft and seemed far off but the way the clouds were moving in, I knew a storm was coming.

I brought the clothes inside and strung up the twine near the fireplace.

By the time that was finished, I could barely see inside of the cabin. It had darkened outside so quickly that I had to light a candle.

I heard more thunder, strange thunder, rumbling on and getting closer.

I closed the windows just as the rain began to fall. Softly at first, then it came down harder and harder, until the noise of it falling on the roof, sounded like a train passing.

Lightning flashed, fully lighting up the outdoors and a loud boom of thunder clapped above me. It was followed by another large thunder clap directly behind it.

The wind was howling and the walls of the cabin groaned with it.

I had never been afraid of storms before but I was terrified now.

Maybe it was my vulnerable state that left me no room for bravery.

I got Hope and we sat down in the corner of the cabin with the dingy yellowed blankets from the bed.

I sat Hope's box down next to me and pulled my knees to my chest and huddled there like that until the storm bursts grew further and further apart and finally became distant rumbles and flashes of light.

When the storm had finally made its departure, I crawled into the bed and slept restlessly. My dreams filled with terror.

CHAPTER 23

I AWOKE TO THE SOUND OF rain on the tin roof. I had no idea what time it was. The storm had brought in heavy rainfall and much lower temperatures.

The rain kept me from going to the lodge to refill my supplies, so I rationed my water and wood much more strictly but I did allow myself to make a pot of tea. The leaves were old and dusty, but drinking it, still felt like a luxury.

I hunkered down in the arm chair with my red blanket and my cup of tea, to read the rest of Jane Eyre. I was thankful for the escape into her world, as the rain beat hard against the windows.

The night came and it didn't differ much from the day. It was dark and cold, just the same.

I made a dinner of cooked oats and beans. While I was eating, I remembered the journal that I had found at the lodge and pulled it out.

I ran my fingers across the gold lettering on the front, savoring the excitement of reading more.

I remembered the words I had read at the lodge.

"So, no one forgets."

I was anxious to know more.

I opened it up slowly …

Her name was written on the first page after the dedication. The penmanship was lovely and exquisite.

Adelaide Elizabeth Harrison

I turned to the next page.

April 23, 1905

As I look upon the dawn of a new morn, my very soul is in anguish, because I now know he will never return to my open arms.
My heart lay heavy with grief.
For the only man that I will ever love, has departed this earth.

My yearning for him will never be met again. My thirst for his love will never be quenched. I am forever doomed to walk this earth without him by side. A punishment for our sins, I am certain.

His child grows within me and despite the shame I am certain I should feel, I cannot help but find myself joyously grateful that I will always have a piece of him with me.

Our love was forbidden, yet I could not resist the temptation of his smile. It drew me in and held me inside of a prison for which I had no desire to escape. His tender hands upon me made me understand what love was meant to be.

I had finally found the love that I had only read about in books.

The searching of my heart had found refuge inside of his.

This love was impossible to understand, yet the very essence of my life abided inside of it. Logic cannot explain the depth and flow of this expression of my heart. It reigned above all things and gave no care for anything other than the sights it had set itself upon.

I had given myself up and surrendered my will to it fully. To the happiness that only he could bring.

I never uttered the sound of my feelings to anyone, as I was in fear of the consequences thereof. Now I must suffer alone in my grief until the swelling of my belly will give way to the truth of my condition.

It will bring hurt and shame, as I know I will bring dishonor to our family.

My beloved's name was James and he was the only son of my father's sworn enemy, Jeremy Constance.

They have been at war over land boundaries and in all of my years I have never known a time when my father was at peace with the Constance family. I believe he hated The Constance family more than he hated taxes. It escaped me how they bore the mighty weight of this ill placed feud between them and where the importance they felt in maintaining it, came from.

I felt desperately ill at the thought of betraying my father.

Alas! I could not retreat from the yearnings of my heart.

From the first time I laid my eyes upon James, was the very last time I was able to steer my thoughts in any direction other than toward him.

I thought of him oftener than I breathed, so much so that he himself had become the substance of my thoughts.

My thoughts now, are upon the future and the child within me, as much as it is on the past, for there is where my heart shall always abide. My heart beats anxiously to think of it. The memories eat away at my inside essence and the tears flow without end.

We met in secret and swam together in the waters of the river, more times than I can count. We laughed and splashed about like old friends. We sat upon the banks of the river, together talking of our future, we now, can never share.

My body blissfully shudders with the memory of when his sudden pause in speech gave way to a soft-ness, as he placed his lips upon mine. We were swept away in rapture, the pleasure of our bodies in unison. A forbidden love had overtaken all sensibility and gave way to an immoral act. A fire of passion burned so brightly, there was no escape. Yet, I felt no remorse or indignity to what we had done.

He touched me more profoundly than I ever thought possible. And afterwards, our love burned ever more brightly.

My heart sang with rejoicing each time I gazed upon his face.

I was raptured every moment of my existence. I was fully consumed with joy and love.

One bright day, he brought to me a gift that I wore in secret. He proclaimed it to represent his intentions to marry me. Even if it meant we must run away together. He was prepared to do whatever it took to keep us together. He gave me a golden locket with a long golden chain. I wore it under my blouse, until the time we would make our announcement to our families.

That time never came. Instead the word of his death hit my ears, like a rush of descending flood waters, destroying all life on its way.

He had been killed by a boar, while hunting in the woods.

My James was lost forever. I would never again hold him in my arms. I could not bear to think of never seeing his face again. To never feel his lips upon mine. Anguish buried into my very soul.

When I found myself with child, a genial light of hope dawned on my loneliness. James had left a piece of himself with me.

I know my father will be angered at me when he finds out about my immoral act and worse, the father of the child within me. But, my father is a gentle man and he will not forever hold unforgiveness in his heart. I know the sight of his grandchild will soften him.

My dearest James, my heart will always belong to you and even as I write these words, I make a solemn vow to never let anyone forget a love that will never die. Death will not separate me from your love. It will be forever in my heart and inside the life of our child.

I will place our child's photograph inside this locket,
as a desperate attempt to always keep us together. I
will wear it all the days of my life.

The rest were empty pages. I wished she had written more.
When I closed the journal, tears streamed down my face.
My heart was broken for her and I understood the loss that
Adelaide felt. I ran to the night table and felt for the locket
in the drawer. I pulled it out and it glimmered in the light
as I looked at it again. I held it for a moment to my chest.
Then, without thinking, I placed the locket around my neck
and crawled in bed.

I looked up at the ceiling and all I could think about was
Adelaide and James and their tragic love story.
My mind wandered to Liam and to Jacko and I couldn't
help but wonder why the world was such a harsh place.

CHAPTER 24

DAY 13 ALONE

IN THE WEE HOURS of the morning just before dawn, I dreamt of Jacko.

He called to me from the forest.

"Mommy!" he cried out from a deep patch of trees.

In my dream, I could see him there but I couldn't get to him. I couldn't find a way and he seemed so far away.

I called out his name but he couldn't hear me calling.

He began to cry.

I frantically tried to get to him but I felt as if my legs were made of lead and I just ran in place. The harder I struggled, the more stuck I felt.

He reached out his arms for me to hold him, but I wasn't there to pick him up.

He cried even louder, as inky shadows moved around him. I watched helplessly as the shadows overtook him and he disappeared into darkness.

I woke up screaming his name.

Sweat poured down my face. I had soaked through my nightgown.

I got up in the darkness and lit a candle. I was still crying.

I shivered, involuntarily. The fire was low and I was soaking wet. I stripped off my damp nightgown and put on a t-shirt. Then, quickly got the fire going strong again.

I sat down in the arm chair and stared into the fire, wrapped in my red blanket lost in thought.

It had been a long time since I had a dream about Jacko.

When he first died, I saw him every time I closed my eyes to sleep, his face filled every dream.

Now, it had been months since I had dreamed of him.

Having this nightmare surprised me and caught me off guard. It swirled me back up in darkness.

It stirred all those old feelings.

The grief.

… and the guilt.

19 MONTHS AND 18 DAYS AGO

It was a beautiful sunny summer day. One of those days where the sky was a perfect Carolina blue and the clouds looked like perfect puffs of cotton candy.

I had just spent the day in Asheboro at the zoo with Jacko and Janie.

We had arrived at the North Carolina Zoological Park at nine o'clock, just as the gates opened.

This was Jacko and Janie's third time to the zoo.

It was only a one-hour drive from our house and I had purchased a family membership, so we could go as often as we liked.

The Asheboro Zoo was seated on five hundred beautiful acres of natural habitat exhibits.

It was visited by hundreds of thousands of people a year.

Most drawn in by the beloved Polar Bear exhibit.

Jacko and Janie loved seeing all of the animals at the zoo but they especially loved the monkeys and the elephants.

This time, they were able to feed the giraffes, which was the highlight of their day.

We strolled through the zoo leisurely, as the children exclaimed wonder at everything they saw.

Around twelve fifteen they were getting cranky and hungry, so we went to the car and retrieved our picnic lunch of peanut butter and jelly sandwiches and apple slices.

We ate at one of the shaded picnic tables that overlooked the lake. When we were finished eating, they ran around in the grass, chasing birds and squirrels, squealing with delight.

I let them play until one o'clock and then loaded them into their car seats. I wanted to make sure they took a good nap when we got home, so I put on the Old Farmer Faye Kid's Songs CD and we sang songs on the drive back. This helped keep them entertained and awake.

Just before we got home, I stopped at the grocery store and picked up a double layer chocolate cake and a couple of nice steaks to put on the grill this evening when Liam got home.

We really enjoyed grilling out by the pool on Friday evenings in the summer. After he got home from work, we would go out and the kids would swim in their floaties and he would grill up our dinner. It was a ritual of sorts. Our little tradition.

I pulled in the driveway, unloaded the groceries and the kids.

After I set the bags down in the kitchen, I got the kids ready for their naps.

Jacko protested immediately. He hated nap time.

He acted as though his naps were a prison sentence of torture.

Usually, I could calm him by tickling him or singing to him, but today he wouldn't be consoled.

It was a full-blown fit.

He wanted cake and to swim in the pool and he wanted it now.

Every time I denied his requests, he screamed louder.

Janie crawled into her bed as I carried Jacko in and put him down in his bed. He kicked and screamed with all of his might, which reddened his face. He was so mad that he had broken out in a sweat and his hair was dripping wet.

I got a washcloth and wiped down his face gently, while he cried.

They were just getting used to sleeping in these new beds.

They were matching twin beds, that we had bought from a shop downtown that carried new and used furniture.

The beds we bought were vintage, four-poster beds made of walnut with ornate scrollwork on the headboards.

I loved thinking of the siblings that must have slept in these beds in the past.

Janie and Jacko had been beyond excited to get their new beds.

Especially, since we told them they were "big kids" now, because they had just graduated from their cribs.

In honor of this big achievement, I got Jacko a *Minions* comforter to put on his bed and Janie got a *Beauty and the Beast* coverlet for hers.

It added to the celebration of this big achievement of sleeping in big boy and big girl beds.

Once I got Jacko calmed down, he asked once again for cake and the pool but this time when I said no, he softly said, "Okay, Mamma."

I kissed the top of his head and tucked him in tight. "That's my boy … you can have cake and go for a swim, after nap. Okay?"

He nodded his head, with sleep in his eyes.

Then, I went over to Janie and kissed her.

"Thank you for being such a good girl, Janie. Mommy's proud of you." I whispered in her ear.

I closed their door softly, as both of their eyes closed, almost in unison.

As soon as I left their room, I started my sprint to get things done.

Washing clothes, loading the dishes from breakfast, and sweeping. I tried to get as much done as I could before they woke up.

I was putting marinade on the steaks when my phone rang.

It was a call from another insurance company. We had been shopping for new car insurance and the phone had been ringing off the hook with offers. I almost didn't answer it but had decided at the last minute to go ahead and deal with the call. I had been procrastinating dealing with the pitches from the different companies. I was on the phone for about fifteen minutes. After I hung up, I noticed the time. It was four-thirty and the kids had been in bed for almost two hours. I needed to go ahead and get them up, if I was going to be able to get them in bed at a decent hour this evening.

I knew tonight Liam and I would need some alone time. We hadn't had sex in almost two weeks and it was overdue.

I walked down the hallway and as I got closer to their room, I noticed the door was standing open.

I walked inside and Jacko's bed was empty and Janie was sitting up in hers.

"Where's Jacko?" I asked.

"I don't know, Mommy ... " She shrugged.

I walked out into the hallway and called his name. He didn't answer.

I checked the bathroom and the kitchen. He wasn't in either place.

I called his name again, as I walked into the empty living room.

When he didn't answer this time, my next thought made my blood turn ice cold.

The pool.

My legs felt heavy and I felt like I was moving in slow motion.

I ran through the living room and out onto the screened porch. The door to the outside wasn't latched … and my heart dropped.

I always latched this door. How could I have forgotten?

I ran toward the pool and I repeated to myself over and over.

"Please don't be in there. Please don't be in there."

I saw him before I made it all the way to the pool's edge. He was floating face down in the clear blue water.

I screamed his name and jumped in. I pulled him out as fast as I could. His limp body was cold and he wasn't breathing. I looked at his face and his eyes were fixed and dilated but worse than that, they were empty.

I screamed. An unmistakable, gut wrenching scream.

My neighbor heard my cries and called 911 and Liam, before running to my side.

The paramedics arrived fifteen minutes later and loaded my baby's lifeless body into the ambulance. I could see them doing CPR on him through the open doors.

By the time the ambulance was pulling away, Liam had pulled up and we went together to the hospital. I didn't speak a word to him on the entire drive. I sat quietly numb. Hoping against hope, for a miracle.

We arrived at the hospital and a doctor met us in the corridor.

I didn't hear the words he spoke. Only bits and pieces.

"We tried everything."

"It was too late."

"Too far gone."

"I'm so sorry."

I collapsed on the hospital floor screaming Jacko's name.

The weeks following were filled with blurry moments of sheer agony. The funeral, his empty bed, the days and nights of horror, reliving his death over and over again.

The guilt.

The what if's.

If I had given him cake.

If I had not answered the phone.

If I had latched the door.

If

If

If

Words that haunted my every waking thought.

I blamed myself, entirely. Which in reality was not the truth, but those kinds of lies seep in so easily with grief.

Someone had to be at fault and I made sure that someone was me.

If only I had just given him the damn cake. Why didn't I give him the cake!? Was a nap that important?! They would've been up eating cake and not napping. Then none of this would have happened. I could've just given them cake. What was the harm?

The night I came home from the hospital, I remember going into the kitchen and smashing the cake into bits all over the floor until my mother came in and stopped me. I collapsed in her arms sobbing.

She stayed at the house taking care of Janie for weeks while I stayed in my bedroom cocoon.

One day she came in my room and told me about a bereavement support group that was meeting at the Methodist Church just down the road.

She said it would be good for me.

I was reluctant but I went anyway.

When I arrived, there were about ten women sitting in a circle of folding chairs. As soon as I stepped in, I felt uncomfortable and wanted to turn around and leave. The door had squeaked when I opened which made them all turn and look. Once they all had looked at me, I had no choice but to take a seat.

We all took turns telling our stories of loss. The grief was so thick in the air, I almost couldn't bear it.

The leader spoke to the group about recovery and healing after loss.

She said I didn't choose this pain but I could choose to heal from it. Immediately, I was enraged. Choose to heal?

Why would I choose to heal when nothing could bring my baby back?

… and there was nothing that I could do to change the way I felt about what happened.

It was beyond my comprehension.

That was the one and only time I attended.

I was gutted to the core.

I couldn't understand how this could've happened to us, when I loved my child so much. How could it happen when I was always right there with them, watching them, protecting them? How did he slip right past me and I didn't even know?

I turned my back on God, Liam, and myself on that horrible day.

It took months before I felt anything but darkness.

Now this nightmare brought it all back. All the hellish, dark feelings had returned.

My baby had slipped away from me again.

I blew out the candle and got back in the bed.

CHAPTER 25

DAY 14 ALONE

WHEN THE SUN ROSE, I forced myself to get up. My head hurt and my eyes were swollen from crying.

I checked on Hope and she greeted me with a loud chirp and a small hop.

I smiled involuntarily.

I ate a breakfast of cooked oats and dried blueberries.

Then, I dressed in freshly cleaned clothes. I hadn't changed clothes in two days and it felt so nice to put them on. They were a little stiff from air drying but they were clean … and that felt like a luxury.

I washed my breakfast dishes, dried them and put them away without thinking much about last night's horrible nightmare. The dark feelings were still there, back in the corner, tucked in nicely.

After the dishes were finished, I took some sunflower seeds over to Hope's box. When I stuck my hand in there, she flew out of the box and flitted haphazardly around the cabin. She frantically flew around and smashed into the window twice. I was afraid she would hurt herself again, so I opened the front door. It took a few seconds for her to realize it was open and she flew out. I followed her out the door. My heart was breaking. I had to say goodbye to my only friend and companion.

She flew out of sight without even a goodbye. Tears streamed down my cheeks.

"Don't leave me ... " I cried out.

She was gone and I was completely alone again.

Just as I turned to go inside, I heard the most beautiful bird song. At once I knew, it was Hope. In true canary fashion, she was free to sing out. Her song rang through the air.

Suddenly, she came back into sight. She flew and landed in a tree next to the porch and continued her song. I felt as if it was just for me. Filling me with a hope that I couldn't explain. She was true to her name. Hope had given me hope, in a hopeless situation.

After Hope flew away, I needed to occupy myself, so I decided to take a walk to my meadow.

When I arrived, the meadow looked cheerful and friendly, as usual. It had become a place of refuge for me. Rewarding me with a sense of peace, every time I entered it. I later realized it was due to the fact it was the only place that didn't remind me of my forest imprisonment. It was a place where I could be completely free.

The sound in the meadow was a full symphony. In the distance I could hear the faint sound of a woodpecker knocking, the sound of songbirds singing in unison filling the air, twigs rustling under small animals scurrying around the forest bed, and the whistling of the tall grasses in the wind. It all blended together to create a song so beautiful, that even a full orchestra couldn't compete with it.

I walked down to the stream and listened to the sound of the water as it splashed and cascaded over rocks into the glorious pools. A little turtle with a black shell was sunning itself in a small strip of sunlight. Her neck was stretched out and her yellow eyes glistened. Her legs were fully extended out the back of her shell, almost as if she was in a ballet lift.

I spoke to her softly. She froze for just a moment with wide eyes and then jumped into the water, disappearing immediately. The big splash from such a little turtle, made me laugh.

I sat down on a smooth boulder along the edge of the water as a deer quietly came to the stream to take a drink.

She didn't seem to take notice of me. Her fine bone structure and big round eyes made her the most beautiful creature that I had ever seen. After she had her fill of water, she quietly disappeared back into the forest.

I enjoyed this oneness with nature. The beauty, the mystery of it all. I only wished my family were here to experience it with me.

For a moment I had forgotten my situation again and had perfect peace. This place seemed to have that effect on me.

After a while, I walked back into the meadow and lay down on my back in the sunshine. The grasses loomed above me, swaying like trees. I watched as the birds flew back and forth. They seemed to be in a hurry, almost as if they were preparing for something. I wondered what they knew, that I didn't.

The image of Jacko's face in the forest, interrupted my peaceful thoughts. The tears immediately began to flow.

The pain, so sharp and so close … again.

I thought again of the words from the counselor at the support group. "You didn't choose this pain, but you can choose to heal from it."

I had rejected that idea as soon as she had spoken it, but now … I thought about those words again … and I wondered if there was any truth to it.

Forgiving myself wouldn't bring him back but not forgiving myself wouldn't change the outcome either.

I was simply prolonging the agony.

I was afraid if I moved on, that it would mean I was saying that it was okay that he died. It wasn't … and it would never be okay.

As I lay there in the meadow, I realized the error of my thoughts. Nothing would ever make it right again. I had to choose to continue to live without him … or let myself die right along with him.

I had a choice.

I did want to live, for Janie, for Liam … and even for myself. I was worth that. Losing my sweet Jacko is something that I will never "be over" but I knew at that moment I could allow myself to heal. I could be set free from the self-imposed prison of my mind … of my own unforgiveness. In actuality, it wasn't my fault at all. Even though, I had felt like it was. It was just a terrible, tragic accident with no one to blame.

I thought of my sweet babies in the NICU, after their birth, as they held onto each other tightly in the infant incubator.

So tiny and sweet.

They had loved each other so much.

If Janie had been able to move on, so could I.

I had already, somehow, clawed myself back from unimaginable pain.

It was time to start living again. To celebrate and remember the joys that Jacko brought and stop re-living his death over and over and stop punishing myself for something that I couldn't change. He was a light and joy to our family and setting myself free would allow me to bask in that light once again.

To start to living once more.

To laugh.

To experience happiness.

All of those things were okay for me to do again.

Once I set myself free, I could be free to sing my own song, just like Hope.

That's what the canary's song had taught me.

I lay there, as tears streamed down my face with all of the realizations surrounding me.

I was free, at last.

CHAPTER 26

E ACH DAY THE MORNING was a little colder and frost grazed the tips of the grass across the yard. It seemed the weather had suddenly settled into winter.

I stared out the window and down the drive. Something I did multiple times a day.

Watching for rescue.

Watching for Liam to miraculously appear.

Sometimes I would imagine that I saw him coming down the drive. Smiling. I would jump up and run out the front door calling his name. Each time, to a crushing disappointment.

I knew he would never appear there. Not now … but my imagination had other ideas and there was no reasoning with it. I was past the point of reason.

I headed out to the lodge for supplies.

The air was cold and I shivered on the walk there.

The woodland seemed ominously quiet. All I could hear, was the rustling of leaves as the wind rearranged them. The dappled shade caused the rays of the sun to dance around me as I walked.

When I reached the lodge, I was tempted to build a fire to break the chill. I chose not to because I didn't want to be here that long and I would be afraid to leave a fire unattended in a structure this old.

I went immediately into my favorite room and returned the copy of Jane Eyre and the journal to their original locations on the bookshelf. I searched and didn't find another book that sparked my interest. I still had the other two at the cabin and they would suffice for now.

I did my usual search for supplies and came across a men's insulated flannel shirt hanging in the closet that led to the cellar. I had been so preoccupied with the cellar, I hadn't noticed it before. Along with it, I found a thermal shirt and pants. I took all three items and put the flannel on right away. It immediately began to take the edge off the cold and I was grateful.

When I got to the kitchen, I came across a shelf of dusty vintage liquor bottles. There was a bottle of *Gordon's Dry Gin*, a bottle with a label that read *Grove's Chill Tonic*, a green bottle with a peeling label, and the vintage bottle of scotch liquor, that Liam and I had toasted to.

I pulled the scotch off the shelf and sniffed it, deciding to take a swig straight from the bottle. The liquid ran through me and instantly warmed me and enticed me to take another swig ... and then a third.

After three swigs, I felt a little more relaxed. I wandered into the main room and over to the record player.

I picked up the stack of records and looked through them. I found a Billie Holiday record from 1944 and put it on, carefully winding up the player.

The speaker crackled as it did before, the music eerie but soothing at the same time.

She sang, "I'll be seeing you ... "

A wave of sadness nearly knocked me over.

Liam.

I thought of his face, his hands, his broad shoulders.

Loneliness surrounded me and I longed for his touch. To hear his voice, to feel his skin on mine.

I danced in small circles alone while Billie sang, with my mind on him.

If only he were here, everything would be okay …

I went back in the kitchen and took another swig of the warming liquor. I fished around the drawers and came across a pack of cigarettes and matches. I stuck the matches in my pocket and then examined the cigarettes. A yellowed, green and white pack of *Salems*. The label read, *Menthol Fresh*.

I took them into the main room and sat down on the fireplace hearth. I pulled one out of the pack and examined it. Dried pieces of tobacco fell from the tip.

I took the matches out that I had in my pocket and lit the cigarette … taking a long draw, like I had seen in the movies.

I doubled over in a coughing fit. I had never smoked a cigarette before. My lungs burned in protest of my attempt.

I took another draw, smaller this time and coughed less.

I couldn't believe myself.

First, I was drinking and now I was smoking too …

I laughed out loud. What was becoming of me?

I finished the cigarette and stubbed out the end. I took the pack and put it back in the drawer. I didn't want to start a smoking habit.

The liquor had started to make my thoughts a little fuzzy, so I headed back to the cabin with the bottle of scotch and the thermals in my tote bag, forgetting to get the water and wood that I had come for.

It was sad to come back to a cabin without Hope there waiting, but I was thankful that she had survived. She was able to return to the wild where she belonged.

I got inside and built a fire. Luckily, I had enough wood to last me for another day or two.

I made some rice and poured myself another cup of scotch. I wondered what Liam would have thought of this?

Me here, drinking alone.

Neither of us were big drinkers but we did partake occasionally. I remembered this one time we were at a Christmas party.

It was before the babies were born.

One of his co-workers always threw a huge party the night before Christmas Eve. He called it the Christmas Eve-Eve Party.

Everyone would turn out and blow off some holiday steam. It was the only time I ever saw Liam get drunk.

The host had made a Christmas punch of ginger ale, fruit punch and vodka. The bowl was placed in the center of the food table. The table was covered in different holiday treats. We had all brought something to contribute. Someone had brought a wreath made of cheese cubes and cherry tomatoes. There was also a platter of breaded sausages, a bowl of spinach dip, Christmas cookies, cupcakes, pepperoni, and Watergate Salad.

Next to the table was a cooler of beer and a pitcher of spiked eggnog.

John, a self-proclaimed lady's man and VP of sales, always dressed up as Santa Claus each year and chased all the women around with his bag of coal. They squealed and ran from him. No one wanted to be on his "naughty" list.

Everyone ate, drank, and sang Christmas Carol karaoke. It was always a lot of fun. Even if it did get a little out of control.

One year, Liam had gotten up and sang, in a not so pleasant pitch, I might add, his rendition of "All I want for Christmas is You." Before he started singing, he dedicated it to me. My face was red the whole time he was singing but I was touched by his shameless show of affection.

He came back from his performance and said to me, "Hey there beautiful, I got some mistletoe back at my place. You wanna go back and try it out?"

Everyone had overheard and rolled laughing.

That got him started, he told jokes and did imitations the rest of the night. All of us enjoyed the free comedic entertainment.

When the taxi came to get us later, I helped get him in the car. He passed out before we were even a block away from the party.

Other than on that night, he was usually a one drink kind of guy. He didn't like to lose control.

With that thought, I drank another cup of scotch. "Here's to you, Liam." I mumbled.

CHAPTER 27

DAY 16 ALONE

I HAD NO INTENTION of getting drunk but the liquor soothed me. It called to me to keep drinking … and I did.

I got drunker than I have ever remembered being.

I woke up, sprawled out on the sofa, with a severe hangover. As soon as my eyes opened, the room spun. I got up, ran out the front door and threw up last night's rice.

I was ashamed. Getting drunk was the last thing I needed to do.

I was ashamed of myself and it didn't help that my head throbbed as a painful reminder of a bad choice.

It took me a while to get going but finally I was dressed and ready to go.

I needed to go back again to get more water and wood. I was using more wood the last few days, as the temperature continued to get a little colder each day.

The cabin would get ice cold quickly, since it wasn't insulated. The icy air seeped in every corner and crevice.

In order to keep it comfortable, I had to continually have a fire burning.

My tummy was still feeling sour from my overindulgence so I didn't feel like eating yet. I packed myself a lunch of mixed barley and oats to take with me to the lodge.

I came up the path and the familiar lodge stood in the golden sunshine before me.

My home away from home, of sorts.

The sunshine had cut a path perfectly through the trees and had made a spotlight on the porch. I sat down in that strip of warmth and ate my lunch. I was only able to finish half of it. My tummy was still not right from my fiesta the night before.

Not to mention, I was also growing weary of the bland flavor, so I left the bowl sitting on the edge of the porch for later. Maybe I'd get hungry enough to eat it.

I went inside of the lodge and dragged a water jug to the front door. Then I went into the kitchen and looked for something else to flavor my barley with. I only came up with a twenty-year-old bottle of soy sauce and decided it wasn't worth the risk of getting food poisoning again. The mustard had been fine but I wasn't willing to find out if soy sauce was eternally safe. In one of the bottom cabinets, I found a small package of *Lorna Doone* cookies. They expired in 1985. I opened the package and there was nothing left of the cookies except a few chunks and some crumbs. I sniffed inside the bag and they smelled fine. I tentatively nibbled on one of the chunks. I was surprised how good it tasted. I savored the sweetness but my stomach immediately rumbled in protest, and I couldn't eat any more.

I put the bag in my pocket for later.

I went into the smoking room and looked at the books again. I just loved being in that room.

I still had the two left at the cabin to read, so I decided not to haul any more back with me today.

As I turned to leave, I looked at the photographs on the wall and one caught my eye that I hadn't noticed before.

It was a black and white photo of a man and a woman standing on the river bank with a stringer of fish.

I couldn't help but wonder if it was Adelaide and James.

Curiosity got the better of me, so I opened the frame and pulled out the photograph, hoping it was marked.

To my pleasant surprise, it was.

Just as I had hoped, it was indeed Adelaide, but the man with her was not her beloved James.

It read: *William and Adelaide Semshaw, 1889.*

He was the one she was to marry ... and the obvious builder of the lodge.

My eyes filled with tears, finally being able to put a face with her name.

I reached up and squeezed the locket around my neck.

I wiped away the tears and hung the picture back where I found it.

When I opened the front door to leave, I jumped. To my surprise, there were two juvenile black bears eating from my lunch bowl. Their fuzzy fur was jet black and their small round eyes seemed to be the same color. They looked like living teddy bears to me.

I quietly stepped out onto the porch.

They didn't seem to notice me at all.

I took another step and one of the cubs' heads popped up. They both scurried off of the porch.

They stopped half way between the wood line and the porch to look back at me.

I took 2 of the cookie chunks out of my pocket and walked softly toward them.

I held the cookie chunks out, clicking softly.

They seemed to be interested but wouldn't take the bait.

Suddenly, I saw a dark shadow in the woods. I could just make out its shape and it was large.

All at once, I remembered what Liam had said about baby and juvenile bears. That was the only time black bears were really known to attack. My body filled with terror. I dropped the cookies and quickly backed into the shadow of the side of the lodge, away from the cubs. The young bears ran jovially into the woods where the shadow had lurked and soon I couldn't see them anymore.

I stood frozen, waiting to see if she was going to come back after me. I involuntarily shook from the cold and fear.

After what seemed like an eternity, I moved out from the side of the lodge.

I saw no sign of the babies or the mother. Thankfully, it seemed the bears had lost interest in me and moved on.

I stepped out into the sunlight and in my peripheral vision, I saw something moving in the woods. Fear zapped through me and down my spine, like a bolt of lightning.

I heard her before I saw her. Snorting, growling, and heavy breathing. I turned to run as she charged me, but it was too late. She came at me full speed. All I saw was a blur of black fur and teeth. The force was like being hit by a car as she knocked me face first onto the ground. I tried to crawl away as she sunk her sharp teeth into my calf muscle. I swallowed my scream.

I tried to get up and she slapped me down with her giant paw. I remembered Liam had said the best way to survive a bear attack, was to lie still and play dead, so that's what I did.

She climbed up on my back and bounced on me. The weight felt like it was going to explode my organs but I didn't move. She stood on top of me smashing me into the ground, as I felt the warm trickle of blood coming from my leg. I held back the cry that wanted to come out.

The bear finally climbed off of me and then she violently pawed me and pushed me around the ground. I did my best to stay limp.

There was dead silence all around, except for the sound of her grunting, heavy breathing and sniffing. I could feel her breath on me and could smell the terrible odor she emitted. The smell was powerful and pungent.

She stood over me and then she nosed me in the side. Then, she pawed at my head, finally deciding that I was, in fact, dead.

She turned and walked off back into the woods.

I lay there for what seemed like hours, not wanting to risk movement, just in case she wasn't gone.

After some time, I lifted my head and looked around. Pain surged through my entire body.

I didn't see her anywhere.

I managed to get to my feet and limped back inside of the lodge.

I went to the cabinet and got out the first aid kit. I doctored my wound the best that I could. The teeth marks in my leg were tremendous. You could fit a full pencil down in the holes. I cleaned it out while biting down on my lip to keep from screaming. I didn't want to draw her back here. Once I had it clean, I took towels from the kitchen and tied up the wound to try to stop the bleeding. Within a few minutes, the bleeding had slowed.

My entire body ached with pain and I just wanted to go back to the cabin.

I was too afraid to leave but I was more afraid to stay.

Close to nightfall, I slipped out of the lodge and made my way silently back to the path. The woods accelerated the twilight and my eyes were slow to adjust. The trees were dark silhouettes and the air was cold. Soon the path melted into blackness.

I dragged myself along in a dreamy haze. I could barely keep focus. The pain was all consuming.

Every sound from the woods made the hair on my neck prickle. My ears perked up in extra alertness. I expected her to burst out of the shadows at any moment. Every crackle and scurry made me jump.

The sun sank below the trees making eerie shadows every-where, deepening my fear.

The path seemed to go on forever, as I walked in a state of shock and determination. Everything felt surreal. I couldn't believe this was me, that this was happening to.

When I finally made it back to the cabin, I made a fire and sat in the corner with a butcher knife.

I was in terror at the thought the bear may have followed me back here.

I sat there until I began to slip in and out of consciousness.

I dreaded blowing out the candle and getting in bed but exhaustion overtook me and I finally did.

CHAPTER 28

DAY 17 ALONE

THE NIGHT WAS TOO short and filled with a dreamless sleep. When I awoke, the reality of what had happened came crashing back. My entire body was racked with pain.

I stripped down and saw that I had bruises all over my back and legs. Where she had bitten me was swollen and stiff.

I unwrapped the bandages and cleaned the wound again. I replaced the bandages with fresh ones from a towel I had brought to the cabin from home. I ripped it into strips and wrapped it around the wound snugly.

My head throbbed from where she had slammed it down on the ground. I reached up and felt my face. It was scabbed up. I traced claw marks with my fingers that went down my cheek. I didn't even feel that when it happened. My ribs ached and I couldn't help but wonder if any were broken.

… but, the one thing that rang true the most …

I was alive.

She could've easily killed me and she didn't.

Somehow my life had been spared.

God, the universe, something had intervened, and saved my life.

I walked away with one bite, granted it was a bad one but it wasn't life threatening and I was alive to tell the story.

It was a miracle and I knew that for certain.

I gingerly dressed and went outside to gather the rest of my wood. I had just enough to get me through another day, maybe two.

I almost vomited at the thought of having to go back to the lodge. I didn't know what I was going to do.

The lodge had everything I needed to survive. Wood, water, and fishing rods, for when my food ran out.

I didn't want to think about it today. I would deal with it when I had to.

In the meantime, I gathered some dry branches from the woods and added them to the fire, to supplement my supply.

As I gathered what wood I could from the forest for my fire, the blue sky gave way to a slate grey monotone and white stringy clouds.

The temperature had dropped significantly.

There was crispness in the air and a smell that I recognized. Snow was coming.

As if on cue, it began snowing. Light flurries at first and then it became heavier with large flakes, swirling and turning, as they fell from the sky.

I quickly gathered the rest of the branches and a few logs before I headed inside.

A wall of ice cold air hit me when I opened the door. I had opened the windows earlier to let in some fresh air and the air shifted so quickly that I didn't have time to get them closed before the cold mountain wind invaded the entire cabin.

Normally I would be enthralled with the beauty of the falling snow but when I looked out the window this time, I shivered, as a feeling of dread came over me.

As I made my breakfast, my leg started aching more, from the bite wound, so I took a pain reliever pill from the first aid kit.

Then, I settled down in front of the fire with the crossword puzzle and a pen. My mind was a little fuzzy but I was still able to complete most of the puzzle.

The snow fell all day off and on. It didn't stick at first because of the still warm ground, but eventually the snow won and it accumulated quickly.

By the time the sun went down there was a thin blanket of white on the ground.

We didn't get much snow in North Carolina, so when we did it was something to be celebrated. School was out. Stores were closed. Just one step off from a national holiday.

After dinner, I took my blanket and went outside on the porch. It was a full moon and the snow was still coming down lightly. I dusted off the rocker and sat down, watching the flakes falling in the glimmering moonlight.

I rocked back and forth, willing with every ounce of my being, for this to all just be one bad nightmare.

I lay down that night and sleep refused to come. I watched the shadows of the snow as they danced through the strip of moonlight that lay across the wood floor.

I thought to myself … if this was just all a nightmare … it was a nightmare, that clearly, I couldn't wake up from.

CHAPTER 29

DAY 18 ALONE

I WAS INSIDE OF a lovely dream, when I woke up.

We were sitting together at the park and Liam had put his arms around me. It was a beautiful Spring day. We watched Janie playing in the grass. A small brown and white spaniel with big fluffy ears jumped around and nipped at her feet, as she laughed hysterically.

The sun was warm and a soft breeze was blowing the leaves on the tree branches overhead.

Janie looked back at me and she was smiling. I smiled back.

I rolled over in my sleep and it was just enough to rouse me from my slumber.

The sun wasn't up yet and I wanted to go back into the warmth and the security of the dream, but sleep refused to return to me.

The dream was so vivid. It felt almost as if it were real.

I lay on the bed, numbly staring at the ceiling until the sun came up.

I didn't feel well when I got up. I forced myself to eat a small breakfast.

My leg was stiffer than yesterday and the ache was stronger.

I took another pain pill from the first aid kit. This time, it failed to provide relief.

By the time the sun had rose, the snow had already begun to melt.

I walked out onto the porch and looked out across the patchy snow. The sun's reflection on white ground almost blinded me.

I looked over to the forest filled with white. It was a picturesque winter wonderland, but I was in no mood to appreciate it. I still didn't feel quite right and my leg hurt even more than it did a few minutes ago.

I went back inside. I knew I needed to change the bandages again but I only had one towel left and I hated to rip it up.

The throbbing in my leg convinced me to sacrifice the towel. I unwrapped the old bandages slowly to reveal my injured leg.

I gasped.

My leg was even more swollen and red now. Green pus oozed out of the teeth holes.

At that moment, I knew I was in trouble.

Real trouble.

This was probably why I didn't feel good too. The infection was already starting to make me sick.

Without a doctor.

Without antibiotics.

I wouldn't make it.

A cold and deep awareness seeped through me. I had to get myself out of here ... or I was going to die.

It wasn't a maybe anymore.

It was one hundred percent factual.

Janie's face immediately came into my mind.

I couldn't leave her alone. She had already lost her daddy and her brother. I wasn't going to let her lose her mother too.

How would she survive losing everyone that she loved?

My body wretched in sadness and fear.

I cried out loud for someone to come and save me.

"Please ... someone ... anyone ... help ... me!"

With my face in my hands, I hopelessly realized no one was coming.

I was alone.

No one knew I was here.

Suddenly, the realization came over me, like the sunlight breaking through to dawn. All this time I had been waiting for a hero to come and rescue me, when I had the ability all along to be my own savior.

All those dark hours after Jacko died, I kept waiting for someone to save me. To pull me out of the darkness, the pain and the hurt.

Now, even here, I have been waiting for someone to save me.

Not ever realizing the one I was waiting for all this time … was me.

I was the only one that could save me.

Truly save me.

I knew I would die someday, that was a given, but it wasn't going to be now.

Not here in this cabin.

My tears flowed and once they did it was like a dam breaking. I cried and cried. Not tears of sadness or tears of joy.

They were tears of release.

Life would never be the same without Liam and Jacko but at that moment, I knew, that no matter what, I would be okay.

I just had to get myself out of this wilderness first.

I didn't know how I would survive the gorge, if Liam couldn't, but I had to try.

It was my only chance.

I spent the rest of the day preparing for my journey. I dry cooked the oats and barley and then made a trail mix with the grains, berries, and leftover sunflower seeds.

I filled my water bottle with water and then used two of the plastic bags I had to fill with additional water. One of the bags began to leak immediately, so I was left with one. I was able to get about two quarts of water in it, I hoped that would be enough.

Once I was done packing, I cleaned the cabin, the best that I could. The searing pain in my leg, required me to rest frequently. I couldn't help but wonder how I would survive the hike tomorrow but I knew I had to.

When nightfall came, I was completely ready to go.

I lay down in the bed and even with as much as I tried, sleep would not come.

The pain in my leg was too strong and my mind was too full. The fear of what I would face on my journey tomorrow ate at me.

I tried to push it out of my mind.

To a safer time, a safer place.

My mind drifted back to the dream I had the night before. All I wanted, was to be there, safe inside that dream again.

With Janie laughing and running in the green grass with a brown, fluffy-eared dog … with Liam there beside me.

My heart groaned in agony. Janie was all I had left.

I lay there the whole night, resting and thinking of Janie's sweet face.

Waiting for dawn to break.

CHAPTER 30

I LAY THERE IN the half light of the cabin, knowing I would have to get up soon. I was excited to start my journey but I was also extremely apprehensive at what was ahead of me.

I was stiff and had trouble getting started, but I had enough adrenalin going through me, to counteract the fatigue.

I folded the blue floral comforter up and put it in my bag with my other supplies. I couldn't bear to leave it behind. I also knew it could prove to be useful to keep me warm, if I got stuck outside overnight.

I dressed in the thermal shirt and pants. Luckily, my jeans being baggy paid off, so I was able to layer my clothing. I put on my yellow sweater and over it I wore the insulated flannel. I was certainly not the height of fashion but I would be warm.

Lastly, I made the red blanket into a shawl and wrapped it around my shoulders for extra warmth.

I quickly made one last bowl of oatmeal and ate it, trying not to think of what was before me.

Once I was done, I walked out the cabin door for the last time.

I wished that I could visit the meadow once more, but I couldn't spare the time. I really needed to make it to the other side of the gorge by nightfall.

Sadness at saying goodbye to the meadow washed over me. It had been a welcoming friend … a refuge for me … since day one.

Deep inside, I hoped that maybe one day I could return and bring Janie here to see the meadow. Though I didn't know if I could stand coming back here without Liam.

As I headed up the drive toward the road, I stopped and looked back at the cabin.

The place I had called my home for weeks.

All traces of the snow were gone and the sun shone brightly down like a halo around it.

This time instead of melancholy, I felt relief.

It was time to go.

The path down the road wasn't as physically demanding as I expected it to be but I grew weary at a rapid rate. My bag was getting heavier the longer I carried it and my leg was in severe pain.

When I got to the car, I stopped for a welcomed break.

It felt so strange and foreign to sit inside of it.

The faint smell of Liam's cologne still lingered and I had to fight back tears.

I plugged my phone into the car charger, against all hope and as expected, nothing happened.

I fished around for supplies before starting back, only coming up with a half-finished bottle of water stuck in the door pocket.

I drank it instead of using my supplies.

As I walked away from the car, I realized how far I still had to go. I did everything I could to not get disheartened.

I just kept moving forward.

My love for Janie was my driving force.

The ground became noticeably rockier as I got further down the road. I stumbled numerous times on loose rocks. I was getting really tired and I hadn't even reached the gorge yet.

As I walked, I tried to not look into the woods, for fear of what I might see. The memory of the bear attack, fresh in my mind.

I was jumpy and the silence scared me as much as any of the noises that I heard.

I tried to focus on the path in front of me, through the tall mountain pines.

As I walked along, I could hear a creek babbling in the distance. I wondered if it was the same creek that ran next to my meadow. I thought about the last time I visited the meadow and the healing I got there. It was amazing to me how a place could do so much good for the soul.

I had been on the road for hours and the longer I walked, the more my leg ached. Then my feet ached as well. There was a burning sensation along the edges of both of my feet, my heels, and on my toes, which I could only assume was the pain of blisters forming. I had on canvas tennis shoes. They weren't designed for hiking, that was for sure.

The more that time passed, the worse they burned, until they finally felt like someone had set my feet on fire. The pain was so intense and I stumbled a lot more than I had been before.

Soon, I saw blood soaking through the white material of the shoes. I wanted to stop and take them off, but I knew I couldn't.

I had no choice but to keep moving.

I stumbled along down the long and monotonous path in front of me. I was numb and empty, but nothing would stop me from getting back to my daughter.

As I walked along, I heard the distinct sound of maracas. An out of place sound for this environment. My brain reeled trying to make sense of what I was hearing.

By the time I realized what the sound was, I had almost stepped down on top of a timber rattlesnake sunning itself in a strip of sunlight on the road.

I had stopped just short of it.

I gasped and held back the scream that wanted to escape.

I was still afraid of attracting anything else to me.

I backed up slowly, trembling, staring at the snake.

It sat with its head raised, ready to strike out at me, and rattling its tail in warning. It was not happy that I had disrupted his siesta.

We had our stare off for what seemed like an eternity and then the snake turned and slithered off into the forest.

I finally released the breath I had been holding.

I was really starting to dislike the woods.

I picked up a large stick, just in case I was to encounter anything else.

After several hours, I still staggered on and there had been absolutely no sign of the gorge. My mind raced as I questioned myself. Maybe I had veered off in the wrong direction without realizing it?

I looked behind me and then back in front of me and let out a huff.

I realized, at my pace, I was not covering much ground. I was most likely right on track and I had just not covered anywhere near the distance that I had expected to today. I had overestimated myself.

I walked on in a numb haze until I stumbled over some loose rocks and fell to the ground, causing even more pain to radiate through my leg. I fought back the tears stinging my eyes. I knew if I were to give in and cry, defeat would overtake me and I had to keep going. I had no other choice.

The cold air surrounded me despite the layers of clothing I was wearing. The temperature seemed to be dropping and it was only mid-day. I shivered as I stood up again. I pulled the shawl around my neck a little snugger.

I walked on, singing to myself one of Janie's favorite songs.

"The itsy-bitsy spider went up the water spout. Down came the rain and washed the spider out ... "

Up ahead, I could see something in the distance, off to my left. My heart soared when I realized it was the lower cabins. I had made it to the gorge!

I stopped right in front of the cabins to take a second break and eat a little trail mix before attempting to go down the gorge wall.

I was thrilled that I had made it this far. It was a huge triumph. That sense of victory renewed my strength and belief in myself.

I stood on the edge of The Linville Gorge and looked out. It was beautiful, indeed. Like nothing I had ever seen before. I hadn't noticed its beauty the day I stood here with Liam after the earthquake, but today I took it all in.

I looked out over the tree tops at the untethered view to the gorge below where the trees stood as mountains themselves. It was mystifying and terrifying at the same time.

I took a deep breath and searched for a path down. The wall was extremely steep and rugged with numerous rock formations mixed with dense brown plants, roots and shrubs.

Each step I took was terrifying. My footing was always unstable. I lowered myself and slid on my behind for a good portion of the way. Holding onto whatever I could grab to help me keep my balance.

Occasionally, I would stop and look at the views, which were tremendous. There was a sea of green below me with occasional spots of brown leaves that were holding back from falling. The expansive views went on for miles. At one point, I caught sight of the river as it snaked its way through the gorge basin. Words could not describe the beauty of the gorge but I knew, with that beauty came a price tag.

My progress was disappointingly slow. All the determination and adrenalin of the morning waned.

The trek was harrowing, every move I made had to be questioned and second guessed. One wrong move would send me plummeting over the side.

At one point, I reached a plateau where there was a fifty-foot drop in front of me and a slick wall of mountain behind me. I stood precariously on a ledge that was only eighteen inches wide. I knew if I lost my footing, it would all be over, but it was the only path to get across from where I was.

I had to risk it. I eased myself slowly and meticulously across the ledge, assuring that each placement of my foot was grounded, until I finally made it to the other side.

I sat down on a rock that jutted out, inviting me to take a rest. I tried to think and couldn't. My brain was numb from pain and discouragement. My muscles ached to the bone.

I looked up at a bird, flying high in the sky, circling, just above me.

I wondered if it was a vulture waiting on its dinner.

Me.

The sun lowered itself in the sky, leaving only a few strips of remnant sunlight across the basin.

I had to face the inevitable realization that I would be sleeping on the gorge wall tonight.

I searched for a cavern or crevice that I could wedge into to give me some shelter through the night. I finally found a place where there was an indentation in the rock wall. I pulled out the floral blanket, grateful to have its warmth and comfort. I covered up with it as darkness ascended on the gorge.

I watched as the sun faded against the mountain and the twinkling lights of a distant town flickered on.

I fought back tears as I thought about how far I had come and even though I had not made it as far as I hoped, I was proud of myself for what I had accomplished.

I lay on my back and looked up at the sky that turned from purple to black, as the stars began to appear. They got brighter and brighter as the sky got darker. They seemed to be suspended like magic just above me. They brought a sense of comfort that I couldn't explain and strangely, I didn't feel so alone anymore.

As the darkness rested down on the gorge, it grew silent until the creatures of the night began their chorus.

Crickets sang, frogs croaked, and an owl hooted from up above, as the wind creaked the tree trunks around me.

I instantly thought of the snake and had to resist the urge to jump up. I knew with this cold, there wouldn't be any snakes slithering about in the dark. Still, the fear was encompassing, as I didn't know what other terrors were out there waiting to descend upon me.

I felt sleep coming, it was not affected by my fears.

As my eyes opened and closed with sleep descending, I thought of only Janie and getting back to her. The insects grew quiet, as the cold settled in around me.

My dreams were uneasy ones, jumbled and hazy. Janie laughing, dogs barking, a woman screaming. Nothing made sense.

As the night wore on, the cold surrounded me, penetrated me. It invaded every cell of my being to the point I had stopped shivering all together. Sleep came in waves, with moments of escape from cold and then back to the shocking reality of my surroundings. When the redemption of morning finally came, I whispered a hoarse thank you.

The one blessing of the penetrating cold night, was that I had not thought of the pain in my leg. When I stood up, it ached with a new tenacity.

CHAPTER 31

I STRETCHED IN THE MORNING light and packed my bag to prepare for the descent down into the river basin of the gorge.

With all the terror and fear of the night gone, and the sun beginning to push away the extreme cold, I felt a renewed sense of determination.

Unfortunately, this determination didn't clear my mind. It was jumbled up from lack of sleep and fatigue.

I made my way as cautiously as I could. My thoughts were hazy and my balance was off. I thought I might be developing a fever.

I descended the rest of the wall in a foggy state of mind.

As I got closer to the basin, I became more alert. My senses were heightened.

I had no idea what I could face down there.

As I got lower, tiny streams of water trickled out of the rocks intermittently, giving them a slimy feel. I was extra careful not to slip.

I made my descent quietly as I emerged into the murky damp air of the gorge basin. The light was filtered with the haze of a fine mist in the air as I stepped down onto flat ground.

The basin was peaceful in the damp morning brightness, and within a few minutes, I made it to the bank of the river. It was a spectacular sight. The water rushed and roared loudly over large boulders.

It was glorious.

I crept down to the edge of the bank where the water spilled over into a small shallow pool and carefully slipped off my shoes. The pain was immense when the air hit them. I slipped my bloody and blistered feet into the ice-cold water. It soothed them immediately.

I was filled with a sense of triumph, as I watched the flowing river. I had made it half way through the gorge!

This was a physical accomplishment beyond anything I had done before. I had taken yoga classes and ran a few races, but nothing compared to this.

After a few minutes, I withdrew my feet from the water and I tried to not scream from the pain as I put my shoes back on.

I couldn't spend much time here. I did not want to spend another night outdoors.

I got up and followed along the river's edge, looking for a calmer and shallower place to cross.

The water was moving swiftly and I had to walk quite a ways down before I found a place that I felt I could manage a safe crossing.

It looked deep but not so much that I couldn't cross, and the flow seemed to be slower.

I slowly slipped into the water with my bag above my head. The bitterly cold water felt as if it would slice me in half as it came all the way up to my hip bones.

I made my way across, moving slowly on the slippery rocks underneath my feet.

When I got to the center of the river, the water was faster and stronger than I expected it to be. I lost my balance and slipped. When I tried to catch myself, I dropped my bag and watched in horror as it floated away down the river.

I made it the rest of the way across the river and once I was out, I searched for my pack. I had hoped it might have washed up on the bank somewhere down the line.

After fifteen minutes of searching, I had all but given up.

When to my unimaginable luck, I spotted it. The strap had been caught on a limb of a tree that had fallen over in the river.

The part of the river where it was hung up was shallow enough for me to walk right in.

I waded in and the water only came up to my knees. I unhooked the bag from the limb, feeling triumphant but exhausted.

I found a place to sit on a rock in the sunlight to dry off. I was feeling hungry and wanted to eat a little snack before starting out again.

I pulled the trail mix out of my bag and found it was filled with river water. I dumped the contents out onto the ground. I figured some little creature who ventured past, would appreciate the trail mix, water logged or not.

As I searched through my bag some more, I also found that my bag of water had ruptured. Now, I only had the one sixteen-ounce water bottle left. I took a few sips and put it back in my bag. I tried to lift the bag onto my shoulder and it weighed three times as much as it did before, with the heavily saturated water weight. I knew would never be able to manage it, so I set it down and reluctantly pulled out the water-logged comforter and left it behind on the rock. It would be too heavy for me to carry.

I turned around to look up at the gorge wall behind me. My heart sank. It seemed completely impassible. It was slick rock, straight up as far as the eye could see.

I walked on and followed the river down further trying to find a place where I could climb up. It was the only choice I had.

I walked along listening to bubbling and gurgling of the river. The morning was peaceful. The sun was getting higher in the sky and my clothes were finally starting to dry. The ground I was covering had been clear until up until now. The sides of the river were now flanked by undergrowth, which made for a treacherous undertaking. I stumbled many times over roots and downed branches.

As I made my way through the dense brush, I saw something ahead in the distance. I could barely make it out. As I got closer, I could see there was something lying on the ground, just ahead of me.

The shadowy outline of it was large.

It was definitely not a fox or a racoon.

Immediately, my heart began to race at the realization that it could be another bear.

I looked around frantically. I had nowhere to turn but to go back and I couldn't do that.

My mind scrambled for a solution.

I stepped forward as quietly as I could in the hopes that I could sneak past the sleeping monster.

Leaves crackled under my feet and my heart was in my throat. Each step I took seemed amplified with sound. I stepped slowly and cautiously, never taking my eyes off the sleeping bear.

As I got closer, doubts ran through my head about what I was seeing. The shape now looked less like a bear.

I didn't know what the creature was.

All I knew for sure, was I didn't want to find out.

I crept as quietly as I could, glancing over at it, as I passed by.

I stopped in my tracks.

Suddenly, I realized what the creature was.

It was a person lying on the ground!

My mind swirled and spun.

A man?

A man lying on the ground! Could it really be?

I dropped my bag and ran up to him.

He looked as if he was simply sleeping but there was no perceivable movement.

His eyes were closed and his face was ashen and purple.

I couldn't process what I was seeing.

My mind whirled with shock and grief.

Liam!?

I dropped to my knees next to his body and began to sob. I grabbed him up in my arms and held him close to me. His body was ice cold.

He was dead.

"Oh God, no!" I cried out.

"I'm so sorry, Liam. I'm so sorry. I love you!" I sobbed.

I coughed and choked on my tears. My heart was completely shattered.

Suddenly, I felt movement in my arms.

At first, I thought it was my imagination but then I felt it again.

I leaned back and looked at his face. His eyes flitted open slightly.

He was alive!?

"Liam?"

He didn't respond.

I said his name again and still he didn't respond.

He was nearly unrecognizable. His face was swollen with purple streaks. His eyes were swollen to just slits. His lips were cracked and split and he had a huge gash down his cheek that had healed over terribly. His skin was white and ashy, and his legs were twisted unnaturally underneath him.

He tried to speak but no sound would come out.

Tears streaked down my face and I sobbed, as I kissed him softly, all over his face.

"I'm here Liam. I'm here with you." I told him.

"It's me, Juliette. Can you hear me?"

He didn't respond.

I laid him down and went to get the water bottle out of my bag.

I cradled him back in my arms and dripped some water into his mouth.

As he got some of the water down, he became a little more alert.

In a barely audible voice he said, "Jules … "

"I'm here Liam." I whispered into his ear.

I lay down next to him and held him close to me. My mind was trying to process the reality of what was happening. How had he survived all this time in the wilderness?

It was a miracle beyond miracles.

I lay there with him for a while, not wanting to get up.

The reality of his condition gnawed at me. We were no where near being out of here and he was dying.

I knew what needed to be done.

I had to get help. Both of our lives now rested on my success.

I whispered to him, "Liam, I am going to get help … "

He didn't respond.

I settled him as comfortably as I could. He was already covered in the survival emergency blanket from his kit but I took off the red wool blanket I had been wearing and covered him up with that one too.

I gave him more water and then put the water bottle in his hand.

I kneeled down next to him.

"Liam, I am going for help. I will be back as soon as I can." I tried to keep my voice steady and strong.

I touched his face as a tear rolled down his cheek.

"I don't want to leave you … " My voice cracked. "But, I have to."

He looked at me with partially opened eyes and nodded in understanding.

I kissed his face repeatedly again.

"I love you, Liam. But I need you to listen to me! Do not leave me! Do you hear me? DO NOT leave me! I will be back for you. I promise."

I stood up and looked at him for just a moment, then headed out back through the brush.

Just before he disappeared from my line of vision, I called out to him,

"I love you, Liam!"

Tears blinded my eyes as I walked on toward the gorge wall.

CHAPTER 32

Liam

I WATCHED HELPLESSLY AS Juliette disappeared out of sight. My body was so weak, I couldn't move or speak.

My heart was gripped in fear. All I could do was pray she would make it to help somehow … someway.

This gorge was unforgiving and one mistake could end in tragedy.

Something, I knew all too well.

Just before Juliette arrived, I had been ready to give up. I had held on for so long, but my will to live was waning. My body was shutting down.

When she first grabbed me, I thought I was hallucinating. It took several minutes before the realization that Juliette was really there.

My Jules had come for me!

I couldn't believe what she had accomplished all on her own. I was so thankful and so proud. I had spent night after night, worrying about her dying alone up there on that mountain. I couldn't save her, I couldn't even save myself.

I was ashamed, I felt I had failed her in every way possible.

I didn't remember falling. In fact, I didn't even remember the minutes before the fall.

When I woke up, I was on the ground and the pain was immense. I slipped in and out of consciousness.

At one point, right after the fall, my entire body became numb and darkness invaded me.

I knew that I was dying.

All at once, the darkness was shredded away by a spectacular white light. A light brighter than the sun, yet it didn't hurt my eyes. Suddenly, all of the pain was gone and I felt so good. The heaviness of being in a body was gone. I wasn't afraid. I felt warm and free. The most incredible sense of weightlessness and well-being encompassed me. It was the most beautiful feeling I had ever experienced. The light radiated with warmth and love. A love that I could not, even now, describe. That love emanated through me and all around me.

While I was in this light, beings appeared in front of me.

Angels, I am sure.

They told me I was okay.

That I was safe.

One particular being came forward and rested his hand on my shoulder. He told me my time wasn't yet, and I would need to go back.

From behind him, two more beings came forward. At once I recognized them. My grandfather and grandmother. Their faces were filled with compassion and love for me. They embraced me and spoke words of loving kindness.

Right before I turned to go, another being of light came forward.

My heart surged with joy.

It was Jacko. He came up to me and held my hand.

He looked like my son but at the same time, he looked different somehow. So peaceful, so wise.

He spoke to me and told me that I had to go back. He told me that his mother needed me and so did Janie. He said, I could choose to stay with him but the best path was for me to go back. He also warned me, if I went back to my body, it would be the most challenging experience I would ever have to endure, but it was a necessary part of the journey.

I slowly slipped away from them and with great force I was back in my body.

The anguish and pain immediately overtook me and I cried out.

My voice echoed in the basin.

I wanted to be back in the light. Safe and warm with Jacko.

I looked down at my twisted legs in horror and saw that thick blood was all over me. I could also feel the bones in my right arm were broken in several places.

Once again, I faded in and out of consciousness. In fits of pain and deep sleep. This went on for several days before I became more alert. Slowly, I became aware of my surroundings and the most agonizing pain imaginable.

The day I became truly conscious, it was bitterly cold. Luckily, I had my backpack, so I was able to get out the survival emergency blanket and cover myself with it. I had the granola bars and the four bottles of water that Jules had packed for me, I was thankful that she had snuck those extra two water bottles in. I also had a couple of emergency drinking water packets that I found in the survival kit. I rationed out the food and water for as long as I could. Taking in only a few ounces of water a day and nibbling on the granola bars. The bars had been gone five days now and I had taken my last sip of water the night before last.

Juliette's timing couldn't have been any better. I don't think I would have been alive in another twenty-four hours.

The days and nights I had spent in the basin were a living hell.

I was alone, injured and vulnerable.

Each night was long and tormenting. The cold and the pain racked my body and kept me from sleeping. The mornings would arise and a fine mist would settle on the river. I would watch as the animals trekked back and forth with their daily lives, never knowing I was there. I saw deer, beavers, squirrels, ducks, and I even saw a heron once. I kept track of the days, by scratching lines into a nearby rock each day. Each day seemed longer than the one before it. The storm, the rain, the snow. It was all a living nightmare.

What kept me going through the long days and nights, were my memories.

Memories of my loving grandparents and my children.

Memories of Juliette.

Meeting Juliette had been a game changer for me. Before I met her, I had always said I would never get married and I certainly didn't want to have kids.

From the day I met Juliette, the way that I thought about life began to change. I began to change. All my life I had been holding myself apart from everyone in the world and suddenly now I was connected to another person. From the moment I laid eyes on her, she was in my thoughts. It wasn't just her looks that drew me in. She was extremely pretty, not the kind of pretty that she had to force. It just came naturally to her. She was smart too. I was instantly drawn in. However, it was her energy that subdued me. It drew me in like a magnet and the more time I spent around her, the more I craved being with her.

We dated for a while before we ever had sex. She wanted to wait and I was willing to wait. That first time, was akin to a spiritual experience. Making love to her was not like it had been with other girls. Before it had been only physical, but with her, it was so much more.

I wanted to please her.

To make her happy.

Her smile meant everything to me.

Juliette was different in every single way than any other person I had ever known. A one of a kind person, specially made for me.

I could still see her face on our wedding day. We were standing in the city garden surrounded by bushes filled with colorful flowers and a hundred of our closest friends and family. She was wearing a long white flowing gown and that breathtaking smile was lit up on her face.

She was so happy.

She was happy because she was marrying *me.*

Man, what a lucky guy I was! She saw something in me that no one else did.

When I lifted the veil, after the vows were complete, I choked back tears that threatened to come.

She was the most beautiful creature I had ever seen.

Her green eyes sparkled in the sun as delicate pieces of hair slipped out of her bun in the wind, falling around her face.

When they pronounced us man and wife, I knew I had just made the best decision of my life. I scooped her up and carried her down the aisle with everyone cheering. I felt like a champion.

We spent our honeymoon in Fiji. We had booked one of those cabanas that were on stilts in the water. We could sit out on the deck and look straight down into the sea.

We stayed in a dream like state the entire week. Making love, swimming in the crystal blue ocean, and eating like kings. It was the best week of my life.

Even our day to day life was great. I couldn't wait to get home after work. She would be waiting with open arms. On the weekends we had so much fun hanging out together. We went to concerts and wine tastings and sometimes the movies.

She was fun to be with. The best friend I had ever had.

When the babies came, I really thought life couldn't get any better.

I loved having a family. Being a dad was the best role I had ever taken on. Unfortunately, things weren't as good with Juliette as I hoped they would be. She was so caught up in being a mom that she seemed to forget all about me.

Especially, once we lost Jacko.

I would never forget the horrible day that I lost my son ... and my wife.

I never thought my broken heart would ever heal and then on top of it, I couldn't pull Juliette from that pit of despair.

I felt so helpless, so powerless, so desperate, as Juliette slipped further and further away.

I sadly wondered if maybe it was more my fault than I wanted to admit. Maybe I could've done more. Maybe I gave up on her too soon. Maybe things wouldn't have ended up the way that they had, if I had tried harder.

I was overcome with emotion. I couldn't believe that I had almost left her.

Those days we spent together at the cabin, here in Linville Gorge were incredible. I couldn't believe how much we had healed between us in such a short period of time. And the best part was that I had actually gotten my wife back.

The old Juliette had returned from wherever she had been.

We were like newlyweds again and starting over didn't seem like a bad idea.

I finally felt like everything would be okay.

Now, I lay here in the gorge, slowly dying and there wasn't a thing I could do about it.

My legs were broken, so I couldn't walk out.

My arm was broken, so I couldn't crawl out.

I was stranded, waiting to die.

After fourteen days had passed, nothing had changed except that I was starving and dehydrating to death. I had not seen or heard a person even once. I couldn't believe that no one ever came down to the river.

No tourists, no fisherman, no park rangers.

Not one soul had been here.

I wondered why I was forced to come back here from the light, just to die anyway in the gorge. What purpose was there in that?

I saw no way out.

My heart had grown bitter.

There was no way for rescue.

No way out.

I had all but given up when Juliette came.

When I opened my eyes and saw her sweet face, I almost believed that she was an angel, come to take me back to the light. Or she was just a hallucination of the mind.

I felt her tears falling on me and realized she was really here!

My hope was restored.

All I could do now was pray to God, to the universe, whoever was out there, to protect my wife and to send someone to her, who could help us.

CHAPTER 33

I FINALLY CAME UPON a place that looked like it could be climbed. It wasn't far from where I left Liam. I could only assume this was the path he took as well.

The thought of this made fear rise up inside of me but I pushed it down.

I was on a mission. To save myself and my husband. It was a miracle he was still alive, but I knew he didn't have much time left.

I was able to make my way up the gorge by going from rock to rock. Regaining my balance with each interchange. The climb up was way more rugged and steep than I expected it to be. I tried not to look down at all, for fear of losing my balance and falling onto jagged rocks below.

I wouldn't be deterred. I pushed on, ignoring the pain in my leg and feet. My entire body was aching, but nothing could get my attention. My mind was on getting out of here and finding help.

I came across several places during my climb that were impassible, forcing me to twist and turn my way up. I broke out in a sweat from the intensity of the climb.

Everything around me was wet with dew and the slippery leaves and rocks didn't make the ascent any easier.

Briars, vines and thick brush flanked my sides and filled my hands with thorns.

Every fifty feet or so, I had to stop and catch my breath. Hand over hand I climbed, as I pulled myself up the slope. My muscles were giving out. The small amount of food I had consumed, was long burned up and I was getting weaker. I was frustrated with my lack of stamina, but my sheer will pushed me on.

After several long and agonizing hours, I finally saw the top of the wall. I was almost there. When I looked up, I lost my footing and slipped. I began falling down the cliff edge, slicing my hand wide open on a jagged rock, spilling blood everywhere.

Thankfully, though, that rock was what actually saved my life because I was able to grab ahold of it and stop my fall.

When I reached the top, my body was covered in sweat, blood, and mud.

I thanked God to finally be on flat ground again but I was far from being through with the gorge. I had made it through the gorge itself but I wasn't out of the wilderness yet.

I hiked aimlessly through the forest, praying I would find my way out. Nothing made sense. I just kept walking in the direction that felt right to me.

By some miracle, I finally came across a grown over trail with a faded sign that I couldn't read. Even though I couldn't read the words, it was marking a trail to somewhere and I knew that was better than the non-existent path I'd been taking. I followed it all the way until it dead ended into a gravel parking area. I walked across the empty parking area and out onto a gravel road.

I practically ran to the road in triumph.

Civilization!

My euphoria was short lived, as I quickly I realized no one was on the road either.

I walked along somberly for a few minutes, wondering how far I actually was from civilization. My head reeled with dehydration, hunger, infection, pain, and fear.

Suddenly, I heard a sound.

Thunder.

Rumbling.

No.

Tires on gravel?!

I squinted in the sunlight ahead of me and I saw it.

The unmistakable silhouette of a pick-up truck that was headed my way.

I waved frantically, shouting out for help.

The truck pulled up right beside me and an older lady who looked to be in her seventies, rolled down the window.

"Well, youngin' you look like you have been through it and then some!"

I couldn't speak, I could only cry.

She got out of the truck and came around to me. She wrapped her arms around me and squeezed me tight. I collapsed in her arms, sobbing.

She had shoulder-length salt and pepper hair with big curls, and she wore a thick leather coat with a wool collar and jeans. On her feet she wore brown leather cowboy boots. When she hugged me, I could smell the scent of jasmine on her.

"Now, now darlin', don't you worry, you're safe now!"

I tried to speak through my sobs.

"My husband …

Still down in the basin …

He's hurt …

By the river … "

She nodded in understanding and helped me into the passenger seat. She grabbed her phone and made a phone call.

"Hey Bill, you gonna need to get some help out here. There's an injured man down by the river, in the basin."

"Yeah, I got his wife here with me. She's hurt pretty bad herself."

I am a few miles off Highway 183, near the old hiking trail lot.

She nodded while she spoke. "Yep, we'll wait right here."

She hung up and looked at me.

"Poor darlin'"

She reached in her purse, pulled out some tissue and handed it to me.

I took it and wiped the tears off my face and then looked at it. The tissue was nearly black with dirt.

I looked down at her seat and realized the mess I was making on it.

"Oh, I'm so sorry … "

"Gosh, don't you worry yourself about that none!" She laughed.

"My name is Della, short for Adelaide, what's yours darlin'?"

My head shot up.

"Did you say your name is Adelaide??"

"Yes, ma'am! Named after my grandmother, Adelaide Semshaw."

I couldn't believe my ears. Was it really her grandmother's necklace that I was wearing? The chances of this encounter were so unreal to me but I knew it was destined somehow.

I reached up and took the locket from around my neck.

"I think I have something that belongs to you." I said as I handed her the necklace.

She looked at me bewildered.

"I believe I found your grandmother's necklace and her journal … "

Her eyes filled with tears.

"I can't tell you what this means to me."

"My grandmother had told me stories of my grandfather. She loved him very much. He died right before she found out she was pregnant." I nodded as she spoke, remembering the words I had read.

"She always spoke of the locket that my Grandfather James had given her. It had my mother's baby picture inside. She lost it in the woods and she was devastated."

"I found it in the cabin at the top of the mountain! Someone must have found it and left it there!" I exclaimed.

"Well, I'll be! Must be fate, is all I can say!"

As she looked at the necklace, I thought I might have seen tears begin to form in her eyes but I wasn't sure.

She opened the locket and peered inside at the same photo I had seen weeks ago.

"Ah, my mother's baby picture."

I nodded as she continued.

"My grandmother married William Semshaw. He took her in marriage to save the family embarrassment from her pregnancy out of wedlock. My grandmother never loved him the way she loved my grandfather James, although he loved my grandmother very much and raised my mother as his own. No one ever knew her real father was James Constance."

She seemed to be lost in thought for a few moments.

Then, she looked up at me.

"Thank you … ." she paused, not knowing my name.

"Juliette … Juliette Bennett."

"Well, it sure is nice to meet you Juliette! And don't you worry, my friend Bill is sending a rescue helicopter for your husband right now." she said as she patted my arm.

We sat and talked like old friends about the earthquake, the gorge and her grandmother's journal.

She told me about all the damage in the area from the earthquake. She said the quake was a 5.1 on the Richter scale and because the quake had lasted so long, it caused significant damage to older or weak structures in the area. She also told me the rental company's trailer had been destroyed and she assumed that's why no one knew we were up there.

I found out her mother had married the very same William Semshaw that had built the lodge that had I relied upon all these weeks.

I apologized for the things I had taken from the lodge and she laughed and told me not to worry, that they were a gift.

Before long the distinct sound of a helicopter roared overhead and soon after, an ambulance drove past us. We followed it into the gravel parking lot where the trail dead-ended. The pickup truck came to a stop at the same spot I had emerged from the gorge.

We got out of the truck and watched the paramedics take a mobile stretcher down into the woods.

The helicopter personnel lowered a stretcher down into the basin and brought Liam up to the top where an EMS crew waited for him.

Another ambulance arrived and the paramedics began working on me. Once, I saw paramedics coming out from the trail with Liam, I left them and ran to his side.

"Liam! I'm here!"

He attempted a smile, as they carried him past me.

I watched as they loaded him into the ambulance.

I sat down on the side of the road, as they worked to get him set up with an IV.

One of the female paramedics had asked me for my emergency contacts and she had called my mom to let her know I was okay. When she returned from calling, she told me my mom would meet me at the hospital and she was bringing Janie.

My heart soared! I would be able to hold my baby again, in just a few hours.

My head was fuzzy but my heart was filled with immense gratitude.

I had done the impossible.

Me and me alone.

Peace and relief washed over me.

Suddenly, a flicker of yellow caught my eye as a bright yellow canary with black stripes down her wings, landed on a nearby branch and began to sing.

Tears filled my eyes.

I didn't know if it was actually Hope or another canary, but I knew for sure it was a sign. A sign that I would like to think, my sweet Jacko had been part of creating. Everything that happened, as terrible as it was, seemed to all be connected somehow, to the bigger picture.

As the paramedics led me to the ambulance. I looked back once more and the canary was gone, but the sense of joy that it had brought to me, surged through my veins.

I finally believed in life again.

EPILOGUE

Six months later

WE SAT ON A blanket in the grass at the park by the library. There was a bright, blue sky with billowy white clouds above us and the smell of spring flowers was in the air.

I took a deep breath and sighed. Happiness washed over me.

I looked over at Liam. He had finally recovered from his whole ordeal.

After seven surgeries and months of rehabilitation, he had regained his ability to walk. He had a small limp but had come out of the accident nearly unscathed, though the scar on his face would always be there. I giggled and told him not to worry, that it just gave him more character.

Liam and I were closer than we ever were before. We smiled more. We laughed more. Grateful for every moment that we had together. Never forgetting the tragedies and trials that had nearly torn us apart.

Especially for me, things had changed. I had gotten a whole new lease on life, knowing I was the hero of my own story. I had survived the unthinkable, twice over.

I worked to live each moment to its fullest, loving Liam and Janie more than I ever thought I could. My heart had expanded.

This was the first day that had been warm enough to come to the park. Winter had held on until the last moment before allowing Spring to break through and we were relishing in this gorgeous day.

The sun was warm on our skin and a soft breeze blew the green leaves on the tree branches overhead, making a soft whirring sound, as Liam and I sat cuddled together.

We had just decided to try for another baby. He was joking around about how excited he was about the "trying" part of it. I laughed.

He put his arms around me to pull me closer and I snuggled into him.

We watched Janie as she played in the grass. She was playing with the newest addition to our family. A brown and white spaniel puppy with big fluffy ears. The puppy jumped around and nipped at her feet. He playfully chased her, as she laughed hysterically.

Janie suddenly turned around and looked back at me … and she smiled.

Just like she did in my dream.

Time stopped for just a moment.

Then, I smiled back, and all at once, my heart overflowed with joy.

Thankful … that sometimes dreams really do come true.

IF YOU ENJOYED THIS BOOK....
PLEASE GO LEAVE A REVIEW!

REVIEWS ARE THE BEST way to help Natalie build her reader audience and your review helps. Also, don't forget to follow her on Instagram and/or Facebook to keep up with news about new releases and see more about her life.

You can also visit NatalieBanks.net to sign up for her newsletter. (your email address will never be shared with anyone)

INSTAGRAM: @authenticnataliebanks
FACEBOOK: Natalie Banks
EMAIL: nataliebanksnovels@gmail.com

NATALIE BANKS

Natalie Banks is an award-winning international author and a previous recipient of The North Carolina Governor's Writing Award. She weaves characters with relatable humanity and stories that touch the heart and soul. She has quickly become a favorite among readers. When not writing, she spends time on the beach in North Carolina with her husband and children.

For more information or to schedule an interview please contact Natalie at:

NATALIEBANKSNOVELS@GMAIL.COM

BOOKS BY
NATALIE BANKS

The Water is Wide
The Dark Room
The Canary's Song

New novel Coming Fall 2018

Made in the USA
Middletown, DE
25 June 2019